Threats against Mary's father were about to become reality.

"Miss Merry! Wake up!"

Polly's frantic voice brought Mary instantly awake. "What is it? What's the matter?"

Polly stood by her bed, a candlestick illuminating the fear in her face. "Get dressed and go out the back door," Polly said. "Hurry!"

Mary pulled a petticoat over her head, then struggled into a cotton day gown. "Where are we going, and why?" she asked as Polly thrust Mary's shoes and stockings into her arms.

"Never mind. Just *go*." To punctuate her words, Polly pushed Mary toward the door.

When she reached the staircase, Mary began to understand Polly's urgency. From the doorstep came angry voices calling for John Andrews to come to the door.

"Open it or we'll break it down!" someone called, as another began kicking at the door.

Mary needed no further urging to quit the premises in haste. At the kitchen door Polly stopped and motioned for Mary to wait while she opened the door a cautious crack.

"They don't seem t' ha' thought o' guardin' th' back door," Polly whispered. "Run for the carriage house."

Still barefoot, Mary did as she was told. Inside, Thomas waited with the cabriolet. As soon as Polly and Mary were seated, he walked the horse down the alley until he was a safe distance from the house, then maneuvered onto the street and whipped the horse to a trot.

KAY CORNELIUS lives in Huntsville, Alabama, and her deep love of people and history permeates her novels. *Sign of the Eagle* is her third *Heartsong Presents* title and continues the saga of the Craighead and McKay families.

Books by Kay Cornelius

HEARTSONG PRESENTS

HP60—More Than Conquerors
HP87—Sign of the Bow

Sign
of the Eagle

Kay Cornelius

Frontiers of Faith Series: Book Two

Heartsong Presents

Many thanks to my fellow writers on the Historical Fiction Bulletin Boards on the Prodigy® and America On Line® Networks for their support, encouragement, entertainment, and valuable information, especially to Kathy Fischer-Brown, Sherrilyn Kenyon, Tom Marlin, John Pickett, Roger Stegman, Barbara Samuel, Beverly Shippey, and Teresa Wakefield.

A note from the Author:
I love to hear from my readers! You may correspond with me by writing:

> Kay Cornelius
> Author Relations
> P.O. Box 719
> Uhrichsville, OH 44683

ISBN 1-55748-564-X

SIGN OF THE EAGLE

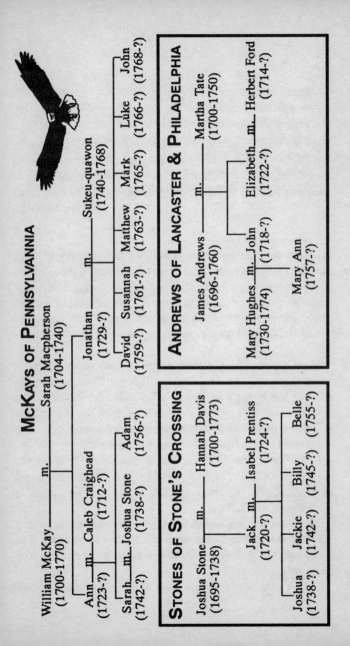

McKays of Pennsylvannia

William McKay — m. — Sarah Macpherson
(1700-1770)   (1704-1740)

Ann — m. — Caleb Craighead
(1723-?)   (1712-?)

Jonathan — m. — Sukeu-quawon
(1729-?)   (1740-1768)

Sarah — m. — Joshua Stone
(1742-?)

Adam
(1756-?)

David   Susannah   Matthew   Mark   Luke   John
(1759-?)   (1761-?)   (1763-?)   (1765-?)   (1766-?)   (1768-?)

Andrews of Lancaster & Philadelphia

James Andrews — m. — Martha Tate
(1696-1760)   (1700-1750)

Mary Hughes — m. — John
(1730-1774)   (1718-?)

Elizabeth — m. — Herbert Ford
(1722-?)   (1714-?)

Mary Ann
(1757-?)

Stones of Stone's Crossing

Joshua Stone — m. — Hannah Davis
(1695-1738)   (1700-1773)

Jack — m. — Isabel Prentiss
(1720-?)   (1724-?)

Joshua   Jackie   Billy   Belle
(1738-?)   (1742-?)   (1745-?)   (1755-?)

one

Even the youths shall faint and be weary, and the young men shall utterly fall: But they that wait upon the Lord shall renew their strength; they shall mount up with wings as eagles; they shall run, and not be weary; and they shall walk, and not faint.
—Isaiah 40:30-31

A spectacular golden sunrise promised a fair April day as Mary Andrews alighted from her cabriolet and surveyed the crowded Philadelphia docks. Mary always enjoyed coming to the harbor, where the ever-changing sights and sounds told of a wider world, but on this day she had a special reason to be there. Her friend Hetty Hawkins was returning from six months in London.

Mary breathed deeply of the warming, salt-tanged air. *Hetty has a lovely day to come home,* she thought. The early months of 1775 had brought various troubles to her family and to the Pennsylvania Colony, but on this sunny April day it was easy to believe that nothing would ever again go wrong.

"Mistress, are y' sure this is the right place?"

Polly Smith, the Andrews' young bond-servant, stood beside Mary Andrews. Gnome-like in her black dress, she peered nearsightedly at the scattered ships which rode at anchor in the Philadelphia harbor.

Mary shaded her brown eyes with her gloved hand and squinted into the early morning sun. "Yes, I'm positive. The paper said the *Sea Pearl* would discharge its passengers and cargo this morning."

"'With a stock of fine lace from Belgium and many willin'

6

hands.'" quoted Polly. Because of Mary's tutelage, the young servant was able to read anything she came across, and she welcomed any opportunity to display her new skill.

"Yes, and the Hawkins family, unless something happened in London to prevent their sailing. Oh, I do wish I'd thought to bring Papa's spy-glass."

"Mayhap we can get closer, Miss Merry," Polly said, calling her mistress by her childhood nickname.

"Or climb higher." Mary pointed to a nearby stack of wooden crates awaiting loading. "Those should make a fair vantage point."

"Miss Merry! Watch out—if y' should take a fall from there—"

Polly's alarmed voice called after Mary, but her warning went unheeded as Mary found a small box and used it to step up onto a sturdy carton. From her impromptu platform, Mary had a wide view of the harbor.

"This is wonderful!" Mary exclaimed. "I can make out four sailing vessels in the harbor, and two of them are discharging passengers. Come and see," she added, holding out a hand to Polly.

"No thank ye, mistress—yer makin' enough of a spectacle fer the both o' us."

Mary looked away from the harbor in time to see several people in the crowd point to her and laugh.

"Momma! Look at that funny girl! Why is she up there?" a child called out.

Mary's cheeks reddened and reluctantly she stepped down from her vantage point.

"I tole you, Miss Merry," Polly said, wagging her head.

"The child called me a *girl*," Mary complained.

Polly's glance took in Mary's aproned morning dress, whose hem stopped a few inches short of her ankles. "Well, y' act like one, climbin' up on them boxes. I tole y' that skirt was gettin' too short, but as usual y' paid me no heed."

Mary tugged at her skirt as if that would make it longer. "It was fine last time I wore it. Surely I should have stopped growing by now."

"Y' and Miss Hetty was allus of a size—I wonder me if she's growed too, these six months."

"I'm sure she will be some changed," Mary said. In the weeks since she'd known when Hetty was returning, she had wondered if they would still be best friends. "Come on, let's get closer," Mary added. She and Polly pressed through the crowd toward the double gangplank which all debarking passengers would have to use.

"Mornin', ladies," a man in somewhat tattered knee-breeches said, doffing his three-cornered hat and moving as if to block their way. "If ye're lookin' for a good man, I'm at yer service."

Mary opened her mouth to deliver an appropriately scathing reply, but Polly pushed her past the man, whose laughter followed them.

"What a rude lot o' men is about these days! Y' can't trust none o' them!"

Mary chose not to answer Polly, whose words reminded her of things that her mother had often said. Mary's mother had died suddenly eight months earlier, and the loss had left a hollow place in Mary's heart that still ached whenever she thought of her.

"You mustn't go to England, Mary—I can't lose you, too," John Andrews had told his daughter when Mrs. Hawkins had proposed that Mary should travel with them and visit her father's sister, who had lived in London for many years.

"You won't ever lose me, Papa," Mary had reassured him. She hadn't really felt up to going with Hetty herself, but some day Mary hoped her father would take her to England.

"Here they come!" someone in the crowd cried, and Mary and Polly stopped to watch several dozen passengers step from a small launch and make their way onto the dock.

"There's Miz Hawkins—an' Miss Hetty, too!" Polly cried a moment later when a group of red-coated soldiers parted, revealing an attractive woman and a blond young lady flanking a splendidly-uniformed British officer. As soon as she spotted Mary, Hetty Hawkins left her parents and ran to her, kissing the air beside Mary's cheek in a ritual of greeting.

"How good of you to meet us, Merry!" Hetty exclaimed. "How are you?"

"Quite well, thank you." Mary held Hetty at arm's length and admired her fine dress and satin-lined traveling cloak. "Did you come back with a whole new wardrobe?"

Hetty nodded. "Some of my old things were unfashionable anyhow, and getting too short—so when Father obtained his generalship, Mother celebrated by calling in Queen Charlotte's own dressmaker. She barely finished this before we sailed."

Agatha Hawkins joined the girls and linked her arm in her daughter's. "Hello, Mary. You're out terribly early, aren't you? Have you kept well? And why is your father not with you?"

It was a habit of Hetty's mother to ask several questions at once, so that Mary never knew quite how to answer. "I'm fine, Mrs. Hawkins. Papa's away attending to some business."

General Hawkins joined them and half-bowed to Mary. "I must say this is quite an unexpected honor."

"Hetty wrote that you'd booked passage on the *Sea Pearl,* and when I saw it would dock today, I was determined to welcome her home," explained Mary to her friend's father. His manner always made Mary feel that he subtly mocked her. She never felt truly comfortable in his presence.

"Surely you aren't on foot?" The general's tone registered his disapproval.

"No, sir—there's Thomas with the carriage now. By your leave, we can take Hetty home."

"Oh, please, Father!" Hetty plucked at her father's sleeve and smiled engagingly.

"Very well, then—but mind that you go straight to the house.

The servants should be expecting us."

The general helped the girls into the Andrews' cabriolet for the brief ride to Hetty's house. The servants had evidently been watching for the return of their employer, for all four had come outside before Hetty could alight from the carriage.

Hetty turned to Nancy, the housemaid. "Have our trunks arrived?"

"Yes, Miss Hetty. The drayman brought them late last night. I put the gowns in your clothes-press."

Hetty slipped her arm in Mary's and smiled. "Come up and see my new dresses. Brew us a pot of tea, Nancy—and in honor of the occasion, you and Polly may take a cup, too."

"Real *tea*?" Mary questioned. Like most Philadelphians, she and her father had not drunk English tea for many months.

"Father had some shipped home while we were in England," Hetty said.

Mary followed Hetty to her room at the top of the stairs, the largest, airiest bedroom in the house. Hetty opened her clothes-press, revealing a rainbow of fabric. She removed a dark blue taffeta dress draped with side panels of velvet and stood before a pier mirror, holding it to her.

"This is my favorite, I think," she said. "Do you like it?"

The dress accented Hetty's blond hair and china blue eyes. Her heart-shaped face and small, even features reminded Mary of porcelain dolls she'd seen in shop windows, dolls too dear for even a prosperous merchant like her own father to buy. However, there was nothing doll-like about Hetty otherwise. She and Mary were still of a size, both slender, both half a head too tall to be considered petite.

"It's lovely!" Mary exclaimed. She stood beside Hetty and gazed at their contrasting reflections in the mirror. Mary's dark hair, brown eyes, and olive complexion had been inherited from her mother, but her rounded chin, wide-set eyes, and generous mouth were her father's. Hetty, on the other hand, had her father's blond coloring and her mother's delicate features.

Hetty waved at the drifts of satin, lace, velvet, and taffeta still in the clothes-press. "Look at these—have you ever seen anything so *delicious* in all your life?"

Overwhelmed, Mary sank down on the bed and watched Hetty exhibit one gown after another, each more elaborate than the last. "They're all lovely, but where will you go in them?"

Hetty held a pale pink satin gown with lace inserts in the bodice to her waist and twirled around. "There will be dozens of dinners and dances in Philadelphia this season—and now that Papa is a general, we're certain to be invited to many of them."

"You'd better be! Where else would you need such elegant gowns?"

Hetty put aside the dress she held and came to sit beside Mary, her expression suddenly serious. "In London, perhaps. If Papa could get into a regiment there, we'd not stay in the colonies."

"But isn't it a great honor for a colonial to be made a general?" Mary said, repeating what she had heard others say.

"Oh, yes—and you can be sure that many regular British officers are furious that he made the rank before they did. But Papa says his reputation will be assured when he leads the Crown's forces against its enemies. Then he can have his choice of posts."

"You sound different—you weren't talking that way when you left Philadelphia," Mary said, steering the conversation away from a subject not to her liking.

"I hope not! London society looks down on colonials who speak with a provincial accent. Mother engaged a tutor to help me master the King's English."

"But now you'll sound strange to Philadelphians," Mary pointed out. "With so much anti-English feeling about these days—"

"Pshaw!" Hetty said in disgust. "What do I care what rude

colonials think? I am His Majesty King George the Third's loyal subject, and I'd much prefer to be taken for English-born than an ignorant provincial."

Mary threw up her hands and slid off the bed long enough to curtsy. "Yes, Your Highness! Your gowns are exquisite, and I'm sure you'll look wonderful in them."

Hetty nodded as if in agreement. "Thank you. But now it's your turn. What has happened since your last letter? Surely you must have a suitor or two by now."

Mary shook her head. "No. A few seemed interested, but Papa chased them all away."

Hetty laughed. "Really? Did he go after them with his blunderbuss?"

"Almost. You know how fathers can be—they think no one is good enough," Mary said, unwilling to disclose the real reason for her father's animosity to several who had sought to court her. "What about you? I thought you might have snagged a duke or earl by now."

Hetty smiled, briefly showing the dimple in her left cheek. "I did meet some titled gentlemen in London, but they were all so *boring*. Actually, to London ladies, there's nothing more interesting than a native-born colonial wearing buckskins."

"London society must be very strange if it admires backwoodsmen, but objects to their speech," Mary said. "I can't say that I've given frontiersmen any thought," she added, truthfully enough.

"Well, do so—we must find out what the fuss is all about," Hetty said cheerfully. "Now, do start at the beginning—you must tell me absolutely everything that's happened in Philadelphia since October."

two

Spring had come early to the Pennsylvania forest. Dark evergreens framed a palette of pastel blooms and golden leaves. Underfoot, the soft forest floor was brightened by maypops and trillium.

Adam Craighead scarcely noticed the beauty of his surroundings, however. To cover the last few miles to Stone's Crossing, he had left the heavily-traveled main road. He rode at a steady pace, but without urgency, his thoughts his only companion. He'd already come a long way from the settlement on the Monongahela where he'd lived most of his life. Adam lifted his head and sniffed the air. The fresh scent of the spring woods now carried with it an acrid pungency that could mean only one thing—a nearby fireplace; campfire smoke wouldn't be so concentrated. The Crossing couldn't be much farther.

Before him a twig snapped, then another. Adam reined his sturdy chestnut horse to a halt, his hand ready on his rifle. "Who goes there?" he called out.

"A friend," a voice answered, and a moment later another rider emerged from the forest and stopped a few yards away.

Facing one another, the two made an interesting contrast. Both wore long hunting shirts and buckskin trousers and were armed with long-barreled rifles and Indian knives. Adam sat tall in the saddle, rangy and square-jawed, with long blond hair and hazel eyes. The newcomer was younger, half a head shorter and more stocky, with Indian-straight, long, black hair and dark eyes. A smile lifted the corners of his generous mouth, and Adam recognized him.

"Ili kelechne, woapalanne-tit," the newcomer said in Delaware.

"David McKay!" Adam exclaimed. He rode close enough to grasp his hand. "So you got to the Crossing first, eh? I'm not 'Little Eagle' any more, even among the Lenni-Lenape."

"Then I'll call you Adam. I'll be glad for your company when I trade our load o' pelts. I'm glad we can make th' trip together."

"I'm surprised to see you here, though. How'd you know I'd come by the woods?" Adam asked.

David shrugged. "I had a hunch you might—and anyhow, I thought I might find somethin' to bring home for th' Stones."

"Are they all right?"

David turned his horse back toward the direction from which he had come. "Come and see for yourself—they've been lookin' for you to get here for two days now."

"It's a long way from here to the Monongahela," Adam said.

David nodded. "I remember. How are Aunt Ann and Uncle Caleb?"

"Tolerably well. Father took a bad cough in the winter and still has it, but he won't give up his preaching and catechism classes. Mother can't do a thing against it. How about your folks? They still in Carolina?"

"Yep. Pa and I went trappin' together this past winter—we had a good year. Susannah and the Gospels still live with Aunt Sarah and Uncle Joshua."

Adam smiled faintly at David's mention of Matthew, Mark, Luke, and John, collectively known as the Gospels. David's younger brothers and sister had joined their aunt and uncle's family soon after their mother's death several years before. "Susannah's near to marrying age—seems like she could keep house by herself."

David nodded. "She could, but the Gospels like it at the

Stones', and Aunt Sarah'd miss them something fierce if they left, too."

"Too?"

"I'm thinkin' of leavin' home for good," David said.

"So am I," Adam said.

David glanced at his cousin. "Why?"

Adam shrugged. "It's time. There's no future for me at Craighead's Station."

Karendouah's face swam before him, and with clarity Adam remembered how she'd tenderly placed the bracelet she'd woven on his wrist, then wept and told him she would marry the son of An-we-ga and Bel-a-ka. Even now, six months later, his heart felt heavy with the memory.

"What're you goin' to do now?" David asked.

"I might ask you the same thing."

"I asked first."

"I haven't decided. Mother thinks I might find work in Philadelphia. Father would like for me to take up the ministry, like him."

"The ministry!" David's sidewise glance and his tone showed his amusement. "You don't look like a preacher to me."

"Or to me, either. Now, what about you? What are your plans?"

"I'll sell th' pelts and take trade goods back to Pa, then I don't know. A lot of our neighbors talk about goin' to the Kaintuck. I might take a look-see myself."

"Kentucky? I hear it's quite a good hunting ground, but I don't know about trying to live there."

"Huntin' like you never saw in your life—buffalo so thick you can't count 'em, and all sorts of game at the salt licks. Land so rich, crops all but grow by themselves, they say. A man could get fair rich in a hurry, and that's a fact."

Adam shook his head. "Hunting and growing food to live

on is one thing—doing it year in, year out for a living—I don't think I want to do that."

"What do you want, then?"

David spoke seriously, but Adam smiled. "To get to the Crossing first and sit down to a hot meal."

"I reckon I can get there pretty quick," David replied, grinning and spurring his horse.

"Not any quicker than me, Davy." Adam urged his horse forward, catching up with David as they broke from the forest and raced toward Stone's Crossing.

❧

John Andrews came home just in time to take supper with Mary. The spring twilight had all but faded, and as he greeted her, Mary thought her father looked exhausted.

"Tell me, Mistress Mary Ann, what has passed while I was away?"

"You hardly ever call me 'Mary Ann' any more," Mary said. "What made you do so tonight?"

Her father shrugged. "I didn't even realize I had until you pointed it out. I suppose certain recent events must have reminded me of the days when I knew the Ann who was your namesake."

"Was? Is she dead, then?" Mary knew she had been named for a friend of the family, someone she'd never met and whose last name she'd never heard.

Her father shrugged. "I don't know. I haven't seen her in years. But back to my question—something tells me you've been up to no good."

Mary matched her father's mock seriousness. "As usual, you're absolutely right. Hetty and her family have returned from England—Thomas took Polly and me to the docks to meet them this morning."

"In the cabriolet?"

"No, Papa, it was such a lovely morning we decided to walk," Mary said, her smile betraying her effort to sound serious.

John Andrews did not return her smile. "You may use the carriage, as long as Thomas and Polly are with you. But I'll not have you going about alone."

Mary's smile faded. "That is not my custom," she said, only slightly stretching the truth. Mary usually went alone to Hetty's, the distance being short, and occasionally to the Market.

"I should hope not! So, tell me—how did the Hawkins family fare in London?"

"Very well, I should say. Colonel Hawkins is now a general, and to celebrate he had the Queen's dressmaker make Hetty a completely new wardrobe."

"I'm sure that pleased Hetty and her mother," her father said with some asperity.

Mary looked down at her plate and said nothing. She knew her father disliked Hetty's parents, from whom he kept a polite distance.

"Do you envy Hetty?" he asked after a moment.

Mary frowned as she considered his question. "I don't think so. Hetty's changed—but in a way that I can't say I envy."

Mr. Andrews smiled ironically. "Life in London would be enough to change anyone, I suspect. I'm sure I'd hardly recognize my own sister these days."

"Do you suppose Aunt Elizabeth will ever come back from England?" Mary asked. "I should so like to meet her."

"I doubt it. Her husband has such a high post that, from what she writes, the whole British economy would collapse if Herbert Ford ever left the country."

Mary smiled. "Then perhaps we should urge them to pay us a visit—I'm sure your business would be much improved if that should happen."

Rather than laughing with her, as her father usually did when

Mary made light of a subject, he frowned. "You must never say such a thing, even in jest," he warned.

"Such a thing as what?" Mary asked, bewildered at her father's reaction.

"As saying aught against the Crown. We may have our private opinions—we certainly cannot help that—but treason against the crown is a crime, and its punishment isn't light."

"Are things really that bad, then?"

Her father set his mouth in a grim line. "These are hard times, and the British seem bent on making them worse. Not always knowing who is friend and who is foe, 'tis best to keep your own counsel."

"I understand," Mary murmured, although she wasn't entirely certain that she did.

"Good. I'm afraid I must absent myself again for a few days." Mary's father rose and came around to help her from the table.

"Not already! You just got here!" she cried. "And what about your promise that we'd go to the Lancaster house?"

"I'm sorry, Mary, but I didn't conclude all my business—I must go out of town again for a short while. But I promise to take you to Lancaster as soon as I can arrange it."

"Will you sign a contract to that effect?"

He gazed down at his daughter. "Who could resist such a sweet request, so sweetly made? Lancaster it will be."

"Or what? What penalty will you pay if you forfeit?"

Her father opened his palms in a gesture of resignation. "Perhaps you'd like a new gown or two?"

"Miss Elliott is already making me some, remember? I know a better one—my own riding horse."

He shook his head and bent to kiss Mary's forehead. "I'll be back in a few days and we'll go to Lancaster. There'll be no forfeit."

Her father had resisted letting her have her own horse for

far too long—whether they went to Lancaster when he returned or not, Mary definitely intended to pursue the subject.

"We'll see about that," Mary said.

three

Adam Craighead and David McKay rode from Lancaster toward Philadelphia, making their way past slow-moving Conestoga wagons and groups traveling on foot. Ever since leaving Stone's Crossing two days earlier, they had encountered more traffic than either of them had ever seen at one time.

"For a while there I was a-feared that Uncle Jack was comin' with us, no matter what," David said as they passed an older couple who somewhat resembled the Stones.

Adam smiled. "Aye, and if Aunt Isabel hadn't told him he couldn't leave her alone to tend the store with all the spring travelers about, he'd be riding alongside us this very minute."

"Uncle Jack thinks that this war business will get worse," David said. "Do you agree?"

Adam scanned the skies with a practiced eye. "I know nothing about that, but I'd say we might run into some rain before we make Philadelphia."

David shook his head. "The wind's not come fresh from the west yet—there'll be no rain tonight."

Adam laughed at the seriousness with which his cousin made the pronouncement. Despite his engaging smile, David was a rather grave young man, little given to making jokes. "Have you been reading Mr. Franklin's almanack, perchance? I hear it gives the weather for a whole year ahead."

"I've heard tell of it, but I've never seen a copy. What I know about weather I learnt mostly from Ma. She could read signs in the clouds as well as Pa, sometimes even better."

Mention of Sukey, as David's Indian mother was generally

known, made Adam feel sad. He hadn't known her as well as he did his Uncle Jonathan, who always stayed with them for at least a few days during the hunting and trapping season, but he'd enjoyed her rare visits. When she died soon after the birth of their sixth child, his uncle had taken it very hard. "Losing your mother must have been terrible," Adam said after a moment.

David compressed his mouth to a thin line but said nothing. *He is Indian enough to keep his feelings to himself,* Adam thought, and was sorry he'd said anything. "Do you know where to take your pelts?" he added after a while.

David nodded. "'Tis the same place Pa's done business with for years. I went with him once when I was nine or ten years old—I can find it easy enough."

"If not, we can ask my mother's friend—that is, if I can locate him."

"You said she writ you a letter of introduction—what does that mean?"

"Wrote me," Adam said, unconsciously correcting his cousin's error. "Mother knows a businessman in Philadelphia who might be willing to take me on as his apprentice—or send me to someone else who would."

"Seems to me that twenty is a mighty old age to be 'prenticed," David said.

Adam nodded. "Aye, but a man can't live without some kind of trade."

"You say you have another letter?"

"Oh, the other's to Father's friend in Neshaminy, where there's a school of sorts for ministers. He and his friends raised the money for Father's passage so he didn't have to be indentured."

"I'd not want to be bound out for any four or five years," David said, shaking his head at the prospect.

"Neither would I," Adam agreed. "If that's all Mr. Andrews

has to offer, I'll not stay long in the city."

Adam and David reached Philadelphia late in the afternoon. The sun lay low behind them and cast fantastic shadows before them. As soon as their horses' hooves hit the unfamiliar cobbled pavement, the animals nickered uneasily and shied.

"We ought to lead them until they get used to these stones," Adam said, and he dismounted.

At the same moment, muted sounds of some sort of disturbance grew ever closer, and by the time David had swung down from his saddle, they were all but overrun by a seething mass of fighting men. Between blows, the men shouted oaths and imprecations at one another, and Adam caught the words, "Traitor!" and "Tory!"

"What's happening?" David cried.

"They seem to be having a quarrel—and since it's none of ours, grab your horse's bridle and let's get out of here!" Adam shouted over the din.

But escaping from the mob—for that was what the several dozen fighting men had become—wasn't easy. It was only when Adam's horse shied and kicked its rear legs that a hole opened for them to pass through, and even then Adam's only cloth shirt was all but torn off.

"What do y' think that was about?" David asked when they were a safe distance away.

"I suspect British Loyalists and Patriots were having it out," Adam said. "Uncle Jack warned there was much bad blood between them here."

"I thought Philadelphia calls itself the city of brotherly love," David said, shaking his head. "Some love its citizens show, bashin' each other about."

"Well, we've no help for it. Whatever they do is of no matter to us. We'd best try to find the Andrews' house before dark overtakes us."

They pressed on, and after getting directions at an inn where they also had a hasty supper, Adam and David soon stood before the Andrews' town house. The three-story brick structure was flanked by others identical to it, but made unique by its bright green shutters. Suddenly apprehensive of what might lie behind the solid oak door, Adam hesitated for a moment before letting the heavy door-knocker fall. When there was no immediate response, he repeated the action.

"Maybe no one's to home," David said, just as the door swung open and a servant girl dressed in black, accented by a white apron and a mob cap, stared at them as if they were some sort of very unpleasant vermin.

"Is Mr. Andrews in?" Adam asked.

The girl scowled and backed away, evidently ready to shut the door in their faces. "We don't 'low no walkabouts here. Go away!" she cried in a shrill voice.

Her action galvanized Adam, who grabbed the door and kept it open. "Wait, please, Miss—we're not beggars. I have a letter of introduction for Mr. Andrews. Is he here?"

"No, he ain't, and neither will the likes o' you be in two shakes, or I'll—"

"What is it, Polly?"

Adam heard another voice, this one much softer, then he saw the loveliest face he had ever encountered. Adam opened his mouth and tried to speak, feeling like the crow in the fable that thought it could sing, but could only croak.

"They say they want to see Mr. Andrews," Polly said, her tone disdainful.

The vision stepped onto the threshold and stood in the doorway looking down at them, framed as perfectly as a portrait. "I am Mary Andrews. What is your business with my father?"

"I have a letter of introduction to him, ma'am," Adam replied, never taking his eyes from her face.

"I hope it wasn't in your shirt," she said, and Adam's face reddened as he realized how disreputable he must look. It was no wonder that the servant hadn't wanted to admit them.

"No, ma'am. It's yonder in my saddlebag," he said, nodding back toward his horse, which he'd tethered to a hitching post beside the doorway.

"Then fetch it and come inside," she said. "Polly, get these gentlemen some refreshment. If I'm not mistaken, they've traveled a long way today."

"What makes you say that?" Adam asked, following her into a dim hallway.

"Philadelphia's paved streets don't make the kind of dust that's on your clothes. Come in here," she added, leading them to a small drawing room off the main entrance.

Another smaller room that seemed to be an office of some kind was to the left of the door. From the front hall, stairs led to the other two stories. Narrow though it might be, the Andrews' house was still the grandest that Adam and David had ever seen. Adam tried not to gape at the upholstered furniture, the leather fire screen, and the lace window curtains, but he couldn't resist surveying the room. When he glanced back to Mary, she was staring at him.

"What happened? Have you two been a-brawling?" she asked.

"Not us. Some people were fighting around us and we had a hard time getting away," Adam said, meeting Mary's direct glance.

Mary stepped closer to Adam. "Is that a wound that needs to be treated?"

Adam looked down at his chest as if he had never seen it before and tried to pull the ripped fabric to cover the jagged, red mark. "No. It's just an old scar."

"What caused it?"

Adam wasn't accustomed to having a woman ask about his scar, and his face betrayed his uneasiness. He cleared his throat before answering. "The Seneca took me when I was about two. This is their mark."

Mary put out her hand as if to touch Adam's scar, then drew back, apparently thinking better of it. "You were raised by the heathen?" she asked, having heard many such tales over the years. *That would account for his buckskins and wild hair and that odd leather bracelet on his right wrist,* she thought.

"No, ma'am. I didn't stay long with the Seneca. And the Indians I grew up with aren't savages. My father saw to that—he's a missionary among the Delaware. My name is Adam Craighead."

Mary looked from Adam to David. "And him? Is he one of your Indian friends, then?"

"I'm David McKay, and Adam is my cousin," he said quickly.

"Oh," Mary said, as if surprised that David had understood her question, much less answered it in English.

"There's refreshment in the kitchen. If you'd like to clean up, I'll show you to the pump," Polly said, directly addressing Adam and David.

"Thank you, ma'am," Adam replied in the same tone he'd used with Mary.

Mary sank down in her father's favorite chair and stared after them. They were frontiersmen, no doubt about it, perhaps the very kind that Hetty said caused a stir in London. She'd seen many frontiersmen on the streets of Philadelphia, wild, bearded fellows clad in fringed buckskin, carrying rifles taller than some of them. She'd always stayed as far away from them as she could. None had looked like this pair, however. The shorter, dark one, was at least half-Indian, she was certain. But the tall, golden one—he must be just the sort of frontiersman that Hetty wanted to meet.

What should I do with them? Mary wondered. If Adam Craighead had a letter of introduction to her father, he should be treated as a guest, no matter how odd his appearance. John Andrews would want that. However, inviting complete strangers, and male ones at that, to use the guest bedchamber was out of the question. On the other hand, the carriage house was comfortable enough—they could stay there.

Satisfied with that decision, Mary called Polly and bade her to make the arrangements.

The Andrews' carriage house, located across a narrow alley from the red brick house, was a two-story frame building. The horses and carriages were kept on the ground level, while upstairs there were a jumbled storage room and an unoccupied room where, Polly said, the coachman used to stay.

"What happened to him?" Adam asked.

"His time was up, so he left," Polly answered. Then seeing that Adam hadn't understood, she went on. "He was bound, like me. One o' these days, I'll be leavin' too."

"This is a nice room," Adam said, noting it actually had a window with glass in it.

Polly grunted. "Humph! Had y' to stay here in the cold o' the winter or heat o' the summer, y'd not think so. Y' can sleep on those quilts yonder. Mice got into the feather tick an' Miss Merry made me throw it out."

"It will do nicely. And thank your mistress for putting us up."

"Humph," Polly said again, obviously not wanting these strange-looking young men to lodge under any part of the Andrews' roof. "If y' plan t' sit up past dark, there's some candle ends in the tack room. But y' must use your own flint to light 'em."

Adam nodded. "We'll not be sitting up tonight—we've had a long journey."

Polly turned to go, then stopped at the head of the steps. "Y' can come to the kitchen for breakfast if y' like, but wait til the sun's up good," she added grudgingly.

"Aye, that we will," David said. He smiled at her, throwing the girl into complete confusion, and she turned and fled down the steps.

"Did you get them settled?" Mary asked later when Polly came into her room to brush her hair.

"They're in Tad's old room, sleepin' on the quilts y' told me they could have. I only hope we don't wake in the mornin' an' find our scalps missin'."

Mary laughed. Taking off her cap, she ran her hands through her thick brown hair. "I dare say even a tomahawk would have a hard time cutting through this mane," she said lightly.

"All the same, those two bear watchin'," Polly said.

"That they do," Mary agreed, but the reasons she was thinking of to watch Adam and David were hardly the same as Polly's. "Please try to be quiet while you brush my hair. I don't want to hear your chatter tonight."

Polly compressed her lips. In the two years she'd been trying to anticipate and fill her mistress' every whim, Polly had learned two things: Mary Andrews was as hard-headed as they come, but she could also be strangely soft-hearted. *A bad combination,* Polly thought as she moved the brush through Mary's heavy hair. Someday it was bound to get them all in trouble.

Despite his fatigue, Adam stayed awake a long time. He and David talked for awhile in the darkness, but eventually David fell asleep in the middle of a sentence, leaving Adam wide awake. He rose from his quilt pallet and walked to the window. Through its streaked pane he could make out the dark bulk of the Andrews' house. Either Mary had retired for the evening herself, or more likely, her room was on the front of the house, overlooking the street. The kitchen was on a lower level in the rear, an arrangement Adam had heard about but had never seen. In fact, he realized, there were many things about city life that he hadn't suspected. Sighing, he returned to his pallet.

Could I live here all the time? Adam asked himself. It would take some getting used to, no doubt about it. Then he thought of Mary Andrews and her dark hair and searching eyes. She was the first woman he'd noticed since his painful parting with Karendouah, and she was definitely a part of the city in which she lived. *Philadelphia can't be all bad if it raises the likes of her,* Adam told himself as he drifted off to sleep.

four

"Have our guests broken their fast yet?" Mary asked the next morning when Polly brought her usual hot scones, jelly, and "tea," made from herbs found at the market.

"Yes, ma'am. The one wi' the torn shirt asked the loan of needle and thread so's he could mend it."

Annoyed, Mary put down her scone. "Oh, I knew there was something else I should have done last night—Papa has some old shirts that he can have. I'll look into it straightaway."

"There ain't no rush," Polly said. "He's got on one of them long buckskin shirts this mornin'. Claims it's more comfortable than the linen, if you can feature that."

"Papa gave me some buckskin boots once," Mary said. "I recall they were very soft and warm."

"But not a'tall fit for a lady," Polly said, with the air of a final authority on fashion matters. "What will y' be wearin' today?" she added, moving to the wall where Mary's dresses hung on pegs.

"The brown, I think."

Polly cast Mary a quizzical glance. "Your silk dress? Will y' be goin' callin' today, then?"

"No, but Hetty said she and her mother will make calls today. I should receive them properly."

Polly said nothing, but the shake of her head clearly expressed her opinion.

As usual, Mary ignored her somewhat sour servant. It was true that the Hawkins might come to call. It was also true that Mary would see the two frontiersmen. In either case, looking nice wouldn't hurt anything.

"I sure would like t' get rid o' these pelts today," David said later that morning. The bundles had been brought inside as a precaution against theft, and their distinctive odor filled the room.

Adam looked up from the linen shirt he was struggling to mend. "Maybe we will, but I still want to see Mr. Andrews first. From what his daughter said, he should be back soon."

"I hope so," David said. "I've groomed the horses half to death an' beat a peck o' dust out of my buckskins. I can't think of another thing to do."

"You might stitch on this for a while," Adam said, holding his torn shirt up to the light. Although he had been working on it for some time, he still had a long way to go. And what he'd already done was puckered and imperfect, reminding Adam of the scar on his chest. *In men and shirts alike,* he thought, *once an injury is sustained, some mark of it always seems to remain.*

"No, thanks. I'd ruin it fer sure."

"Someone's coming," Adam said, hearing footsteps on the coach house stairs.

As Polly entered the room, David stood and bowed low. "Good mornin', Miss Polly," he said pleasantly, bringing a blushing scowl to the servant's face.

"Mistress Andrews will see you at your pleasure," she said, addressing Adam.

"Myself alone?" he questioned.

"The both o' you, I suppose. But hurry on now—Miss Mary's expectin' quality company in a little while."

"We'll be there right away," Adam said.

"Quality company?" David questioned when Polly had left. "What does *that* mean?"

Adam laughed and rose, laying the shirt aside. "It means that Miss Polly doesn't think much of us."

"What about her mistress?"

Adam shrugged. "She let us stay here last night—she must see some good in us."

"Still, we ought to plan to move on. I don't want to be beholden to anyone, much less a female."

"You're right. But for now, cousin, we mustn't keep the lady waiting."

When Adam and David appeared in the drawing room doorway, Mary stood and handed Adam a cloth-wrapped bundle. "I should have given you these last night," she said, her soft brown eyes meeting his. "They are my father's—I hope you can wear them."

Adam opened the bundle and took out a shirt. Holding it up, he saw that it was made of fine lawn, but also that it was far shorter than the shirt he'd been mending.

"I appear to be some taller than your father, who might not want you to give away his shirts in any case," Adam said. He handed the bundle back to Mary, who gestured for Polly to take it. Mary's face reddened, and Adam hoped his refusal hadn't angered her.

"Yes, I suppose you are some taller," she said.

"When can we see your father?" Adam asked.

"I'm not sure," Mary said. "He—"

Mary broke off speaking as the door knocker sounded.

"David and I will leave now," Adam said as Polly swept past them to answer the door, casting a meaningful glance in their direction. "We have some other calls to make, then we'll stop by later. Perhaps Mr. Andrews will be back by then."

"Don't go!" Mary said. She could hear Hetty's voice, and Mary knew her friend would never forgive her if she didn't let her meet these genuine frontiersmen.

Adam had turned to leave, but stopped at her words. "We can't impose—" he began, but then Hetty and her father were in the hall, and it was too late for him and David to leave gracefully.

"General Hawkins, what a surprise!" Mary said in a bright tone of voice far different from what she had used with Adam and David. "Hetty, dear, how did you manage to get your father to come with you to call?"

"The same way she gets me to do anything," General Hawkins said. "Those blue eyes of hers can be very persuasive."

"Oh, Papa!" Hetty said. Then she turned and saw Adam and David and her mouth fell open in surprise. She looked back to Mary and waited to be introduced.

"General Hawkins, Hetty—may I present Adam Craighead and David—"

"McKay," David supplied, and again Mary was embarrassed that she hadn't recalled his name.

Adam noted that the general's eyes were as blue as his daughter's, and that he was tall and well-built, resplendent in his new, bright red uniform, trimmed with gold braid. There was an awkward moment before General Hawkins extended his hand, first to Adam, and then to David.

"Craighead and McKay, eh?" he said. "From around the Monongahela, perhaps?"

"I am, sir," Adam replied. "David lives in North Carolina."

"Won't you sit down?" Mary invited, gesturing toward the drawing room.

Everyone followed Mary into the drawing room, where David and Adam sat together on a sofa. The general sat opposite them, while Hetty and Mary seated themselves in wing chairs flanking the sofa.

General Hawkins leaned forward and looked closely at Adam and David. "I believe I might know your father," he said to David. "Did he ever hunt around Fort Bedford?"

"Yes, sir—all through that area. He's a hunter to this day."

"And you, young man—from your garb, I presume you

hunt, as well?"

"Not for a living," Adam said.

"Perhaps you'd both be interested in signing on with the British Army, then." General Hawkins looked directly at David. "Am I right in assuming you have Indian blood?"

"My mother was from the Delaware," David said.

The general looked pleased. "I thought so! I had charge of Fort Bedford in '58. Later I recruited and trained native troops to defend against the French. Splendid fighters they were. I should like to do the same thing again. Someone like you, intimately bound by blood to the Indians' language and customs, would be invaluable to the Crown."

"I'm not a soldier, sir," David McKay said levelly. "I've no interest in makin' war."

"It's not a matter of interest, but of patriotism," General Hawkins said. "We're all subjects of His Majesty the King. The colonies are merely branches of Britain, which has spent a great deal of money and effort on providing them with its protection."

"Oh, Papa, please don't start a tiresome lecture!" Hetty exclaimed.

"A lecture? Nonsense! I am merely making a legitimate offer of employment to some fellows who look as though they could use it."

"Thank you, sir, but we don't need your help," Adam said, trying hard to be polite for Mary's sake. He had no experience with Philadelphia drawing rooms, but he knew that a man shouldn't insult another when both are guests of a lady. Not even the worst of the "savages" he had been raised among would be so crude.

"Mr. Craighead has a letter of introduction for my father," Mary said quickly.

General Hawkins looked back to Adam and frowned as if trying to remember something. "Craighead—seems I've heard the name before."

"My father is a missionary among the Delaware," Adam offered. "Perhaps you've heard of his work."

"No, it wasn't that—" General Hawkins furrowed his brow, then shook his head. "I'll not rest until I can recall the connection, but for now, it eludes me."

"I have an older sister named Sarah. She once stayed at Fort Bedford during the trouble with the French. Perhaps you met her then," Adam said.

General Hawkins' face cleared and he nodded. "Of course! Sarah Craighead—came to Bedford dressed like an Indian—a pretty young woman. As I recall, she was on her way to some Crossing or Station. Where is she now?"

"In North Carolina with her husband, Joshua Stone. He was with her at the fort, I believe."

"Yes, I recall such a man, although I had forgot the name. Well, young men, I repeat my offer. You must know that I am in a position to secure you both good postings with His Majesty's troops."

No one said anything for a moment, then David spoke. "Much obliged, sir, but as a matter of fact, I've not decided whose side I'd be on if it came to a fight. I'd best stay away from anyone's army for now."

"And you, Mr. Craighead? Are your sentiments the same?"

Adam matched the general's direct gaze. "They are."

"Then there is nothing more to say." General Hawkins' voice was distinctly cool.

Recognizing they were being summarily dismissed, Adam and David stood and bowed to the ladies before taking their leave.

Mary followed them into the hall and laid a restraining hand on Adam's sleeve, her voice urgent. "Don't leave yet—my father would be very upset to find that I had let you get away."

"Thank you, ma'am, but we're not fish to be reeled in. I

think it best for us to move on," Adam said.

"At least stay here another night," Mary begged. "One more night—then if Papa still hasn't come home, you may go."

"What about it, David?" Adam asked. He turned to his cousin, who shrugged.

"I reckon we can stay—as long as I don't have to see *him* again," David said, nodding in the direction of General Hawkins.

Mary looked pleased. "Polly will call you to supper. Goodbye for now."

As Mary returned to her guests, Adam and David went back to the carriage house.

"I wouldn't work for that man for a pile of gold," David said.

"Neither would I," Adam agreed. "I hope we don't run into him again."

David glanced knowingly at Adam. "One member of that family'd like to see y' again, though."

"I don't know what you're talking about."

"That Miss Hetty's got the bluest eyes I ever saw—and she never took 'em off you, even for a second."

Adam shook his head. "I think you're daft," he said flatly.

But on one thing he had to agree with David. Hetty Hawkins did, indeed, have exceedingly blue eyes.

five

"You mustn't let that pair get away, Mary."

General Hawkins had gone on to make some calls of his own, leaving his daughter with Mary, and Hetty wasted no time in broaching the subject of the men she'd just met.

Mary Andrews frowned. "They're not animals in a menagerie, you know. If Papa doesn't come back today, I've no doubt they'll leave."

"The tall one—Adam, you said? If he has a letter of introduction, he'll be back."

"He said he did, but I never actually saw it—he might just be pretending."

"Why would he do that? If they were going to rob you they would already have done so. Besides, they don't look like the criminal sort."

Mary smiled briefly. "Thieves seldom advertise their intentions, Hetty. But I agree—they didn't come to rob us. If I knew where Papa was staying, I'd send after him."

Hetty idly twisted a golden curl around her finger. "So your father still takes mysterious trips—have you ever found out why?"

Mary looked away from Hetty's piercing blue eyes and shook her head. "As a matter of fact, I haven't asked," she said, telling a partial truth. Mary hadn't asked because she'd been told not to—but she knew more about her father's errands than she dared to tell Hetty. "Anyway, what would you do with the frontiersmen if they decided to stay in Philadelphia?"

Hetty smiled, displaying her dimple. "Why, I'd introduce them to society, of course. Wouldn't their buckskins look

36

wonderful in the midst of all the ruffled and stuffed shirts at the next cotillion?"

Mary winced at the thought. "I doubt very much if either of that pair would willingly attend such an event—and even if they did, they'd certainly know better than to wear buckskins."

Hetty's lips curved in a slight smile. "But that would spoil the fun," she said.

"They wouldn't find it at all entertaining," Mary replied.

"Perhaps not, but I certainly would," Hetty said. "And the way you're rushing to defend them tells me that Mistress Merry has more than a passing interest in the matter herself."

"You are quite mistaken, my dear," Mary said, attempting to sound like a haughty English grande dame and succeeding only in making Hetty laugh.

"Ah, now you sound like the Merry Andrews I remember. How I missed your quick wit all those months!"

With the subject safely away from the frontiersmen, Mary smiled back at Hetty and rose. "Come now and see my new gowns. They're not as grand as yours, but you can tell me which I ought to wear to your father's gala."

⋙

"I don't think Mistress Mary has any idea when her father will be back," Adam told David that evening when once more John Andrews had failed to appear. They had just returned to the carriage house after taking supper in the kitchen, where Polly had informed them that her mistress was dining with friends, then had hovered over them throughout the meal as if she feared they might otherwise steal the plates.

"I thought so from the first," David said, "yet she seems t' want t' keep us about. Odd girl, she is."

"Oh, I don't know about that," Adam said. "Perhaps she really is trying to do what she thinks her father would want. But I agree that it's time we moved on. First thing tomorrow, we'll take your pelts to market. Then I'll find the Reverend

Ian MacPherson."

David nodded. "Pa's countin' on me t' get a fair price for the pelts. If you're with me, I'm not as like to get cheated."

Adam looked amused. "Why? I've never traded pelts in my life."

"No, but you look like you have, an' sometimes that's all that matters."

"Appearances aren't everything," Adam said, thinking not just about David's business transaction, but about the strange girl who had offered them a distant hospitality.

What does Mary Andrews really think about us? Adam wondered. But he was careful not to ask himself if he cared.

‰

"Tell Miss Andrews that we'll be back later," Adam told Polly the next morning as he and David prepared to leave. They made their way through Philadelphia's wide streets, already thronged with market-goers, to a row house where a single sign bearing a crude representation of a beaver pelt signaled the place of business that David sought.

A bell attached to the door tinkled as they opened it, and the unmistakable odor of animal skins assailed them as they stepped inside. Robbie McCall, the white-haired broker David's father had dealt with for years, greeted David with hearty affection and insisted that he report all the family news before he'd even look at David's bundles.

"'Tis good t' see ye again and a pleasure t' meet your cousin. Sit down, make yourself to home. Alex! Come and make a place for these lads to sit."

McCall's apprentice, a sullen, dark-skinned boy wrapped in a stained leather apron, appeared from the back room and gathered up several pelt bundles from the only other chairs in the office.

"So, young man, will ye be followin' after yer father in the trade now?"

"No, sir," David replied. "I intend to do something different."

"Different, is it?" McCall leaned back in his chair and looked appraisingly at David. "Well, ye're not a big 'un, but ye seem strong enough. Are ye come to seek work in the city, then?"

David shook his head. "No, sir. From what I've seen, I don't think I'd take kindly to city life."

McCall nodded, unsurprised. "Might ye be givin' some thought to the army, then?"

"Nay, I've no interest in makin' a soldier."

"And you?" McCall asked, turning to Adam. "Dozens of frontiersmen are comin' to Philadelphia every day, signin' up on one side or another. I'm sure they'd welcome such a strappin' young man as yerself. I hear the British are offerin' fine bounties these days."

From the questioning tone in his voice, Adam understood that McCall wanted to know where his loyalties lay without giving away his own. "Neither of us came here to fight anyone," he said.

McCall's eyes held Adam's for a long moment, then he nodded as if he understood something Adam had left unsaid. "Still, ye may find ye have no choice. The time is comin' when every colonial will have t' choose sides."

"It seems that time may already have come—as soon as David and I reached the city yesterday, we got caught up in a brawl that seemed to be between Patriots and Loyalists."

"Aye, such clashes are commonplace these days. My advice to ye both is t' consider which side ye'll take when th' fightin' starts in earnest—an' mark my words, that time's a-comin', sooner than any of us might want."

Seeing the serious expressions his words had brought to Adam and David, McCall stood and put his hand on David's shoulder. "But that's enough of an old man's rantin'. Come now and let's have a look at those pelts ye brought."

Mary was disappointed when Polly told her that Adam and David had gone off practically at dawn and left no word when they would be returning. As soon as she dressed, Mary went to the carriage house to satisfy herself that their things were still there. While there, she noticed the linen shirt that Adam had tried to mend.

"Polly, find my sewing basket, please," she called when she came back into the house bearing the shirt.

"Surely you ain't gonna work on that rag!" Polly exclaimed, warily eyeing Adam's garment.

"Somebody needs to," Mary replied. "Adam Craighead may be quite at home in the wilderness, but he knows nothing about sewing."

Polly sniffed. "An' why should he, when a lady of quality lowers herself to take on the task?"

Mary shot an exasperated look at Polly, whose notions about proper society were far different from her own. "Since when does performing a service lower anyone? Do you not recall that even our Lord washed His disciples' feet?"

"I also remember Mr. John sayin' that even Satan can quote Scripture," Polly muttered.

"Oh, I'm Satan now, am I?" Mary teased, and reluctantly Polly's mouth twitched in a near-smile.

"Don't twist my words, Miss Merry. You may trust that pair o' buckskins, but I'll rest me easier when they've gone on their way."

"I'm sure that won't be much longer—but in the meantime, I see nothing wrong in seeing that Adam Craighead has at least one decent shirt."

At McCall's insistence, Adam and David took lunch with him at a popular establishment only a few doors from the peltry business. When questioned about why part of its sign had been painted out, leaving only the word "Stag" under a picture of a large buck deer, McCall explained that the owner had thought it prudent to remove the "Royal" that had preceded it.

"When he put it up, the British had just chased away the French, and nothin' was too good for His Majesty's troops. Every store owner in town wanted to get some sort o' British symbol on his sign."

"Now that y' mention it, I don't think we've seen many such symbols since we've come, have we, Adam?" David said.

"Not that I recall, but then we weren't looking for any," Adam said.

"Oh, there's still some about, lots of places where the Loyals gather," McCall said. "But I say a man needs a place t' get a good joint o' meat and a hunk o' bread wi'out havin' t' talk politics—and the Stag is just th' place. Eat hearty, lads."

Between McCall's penchant for story-telling and the dozens of men who stopped by the plank table to talk to the peltry merchant, it was far into the afternoon before Adam and David parted with McCall. At the merchant's advice, they bought a thin leather strip for David to wrap the peltry money in and hide beneath his hunting shirt.

"Philadelphia's as full as thieves as fleas on a dog," McCall warned them. "Put a reg'lar wampum belt on the outside o' your shirt and next thing y' know, it's cut off an' yer money's gone. And don't get the trade goods until yer ready to go back, neither, less'n yer willin' t' sleep wi' one eye open all the time."

"The more I hear about Philadelphia, the less I like it," David said as they made their way back to the street where John and Mary Andrews lived. "I can't imagine that anybody'd want t' live here."

"McCall knows that visitors are often taken advantage of. The people who live here don't seem to be afraid for their lives."

"Well, they don't seem all that friendly, either, 'cept for McCall, and in his case it's prob'ly just good business t' be nice to us. I'm ready to move on from here, myself."

Adam nodded. "All right. If John Andrews still isn't at home, we'll go on to Neshaminy tonight."

"I'll go 'round and pack up our gear," David said when they reached the house.

"I'll see if he's here, then I'll join you," Adam said.

When Mary opened the front door to admit him, the look on her face told Adam that her father still hadn't returned.

"You and your friend are welcome to stay in the carriage house as long as you like," she added after confirming her father's absence.

"I hope nothing has happened to him," Adam said, reading the concern expressed in her eyes. "The peltry merchant warned us to watch out for thieves."

Mary's reddened cheeks baffled Adam. "I'm not worried about his safety," she said. "I just thought that he'd be here by now. I know you must have other matters to attend to."

"Yes, we do. As a matter of fact, we must go on to Neshaminy this evening."

Mary looked surprised. "But soon it'll be supper time, and it's a long way to Neshaminy. At least stay the night."

"No, we can't. You've done enough for us already."

"It was no more than my father would have wanted," Mary said quickly, avoiding looking at Adam directly. "Before you go, I have something to give you. Wait here—I'll be right back."

Adam stood in the hallway and admired Mary's grace as she mounted the stairs. She returned only moments later, holding something white.

"Your shirt," she said, handing it to him.

He looked in surprise at the garment, which had been neatly mended with almost invisible stitches. "How came you by this?" he asked, bringing faint color to her cheeks.

"I went to the carriage house this morning to see if you'd taken your things with you. I couldn't help but see that the shirt needed a woman's hand."

I ought to tell her she has no business meddling in my possessions, Adam thought, but he couldn't reject Mary's gesture of good will. "I'm afraid you're right," he said instead. "Thank you—or should I thank Polly?"

Mary raised her chin slightly and looked him in the eyes. "Polly can't sew as well as you. No, Mr. Craighead, these did every stitch."

She extended her hands, spreading her fingers as if to prove that she was, indeed, a capable seamstress. Without stopping to think about how it might be taken, Adam took her hands in his and held them. Mary looked startled, but she made no move to pull away from his grasp.

"David and I do appreciate your welcome, Miss Andrews," he said. "And perhaps we'll yet be able to convey our respects to your father."

"How long will you stay at Neshaminy?" Mary asked.

"A day or two, perhaps. A friend of my father's lives there," he added, then chastised himself for appearing to presume that she cared.

"You must come back here before you leave Philadelphia. My father will be home soon—perhaps this very evening."

Adam watched Mary's expression closely and wondered if she could read his expression as well as he read hers. *She's not just being polite,* he realized, and the thought so unsettled him that he dropped her hands as if they had suddenly become burning coals.

"Tell him I'm sorry I missed seeing him," he murmured, then turned to go, too embarrassed to see the effect of his strange behavior on Mary.

"Wait!" Mary called out, and Adam stopped and turned to

face her again.

"What is it?" he asked.

"Shall I tell my father that you'll be back, then?"

Once more their eyes met, and Adam nodded, his throat suddenly tight. "Yes, I'll be back. But if he isn't here, I must go on."

"I understand," Mary said. Then her expression brightened. "Why don't you leave your letter of introduction here? I'll give it to my father as soon as he comes back."

Why didn't I think of that? Adam thought. "I suppose I could," he said aloud. His letter of introduction to John Andrews would mean nothing to anyone else. "I'll give it to you before we go."

I'll see him once more, at any rate, Mary thought as Adam left her. And if the letter didn't bear a seal, she might even find out just what it was that Adam Craighead wanted from her father.

six

"Are you ready to go now?" David asked Adam when he entered the room over the carriage house. He had folded the quilts neatly and their packed saddle bags lay by the stairs. Without the bundles of pelts, their possessions now seemed meager.

Adam nodded. "Yes, after I find that letter to John Andrews. Miss Andrews offered to give it to him for me."

David grinned. "What else did she offer? She wanted us to stay around longer, too, didn't she?"

"She extended her original offer of hospitality, if that's what you mean," Adam said, determined to ignore his cousin's teasing. "She also said Polly would be heart-broken when you left."

David threw his head back and laughed. "Aye, Adam, y' know 'tis a sin t' lie like that—y' ought t' be ashamed!"

Adam assumed an expression of mock solemnity. "And ashamed I would be, but the fact is, that girl has her eye on you, cousin. The least you can do is give her a proper farewell and thank her for waiting on us these two days."

David's smile faded. "Aye, she's fussed and grumbled, but she's fed us well, and we're bound t' have made more work. But such thanks are best come from you. I've not got your gift o' fair talkin'."

"I have no such gift that I know of," Adam said. "But I will tell Polly and our hostess that you are properly grateful. Now, if I can just find that letter—"

A few minutes later, letter in hand, Adam went to the rear door, where Polly greeted him as if unsurprised that their guests were going. Mary sat in the drawing room, making tiny stitches in what appeared to be some sort of coverlet.

"Don't disturb yourself, ma'am," Adam said when Mary started to rise when she saw him. "I'll just leave this letter on the table. David asked me to thank you and Miss Polly for taking us in. We'll be on our way now, before the day gets older."

Mary looked as if she wanted to say something more, but with Polly hovering behind Adam, apparently eager to see him and David on their way, she merely nodded and repeated her invitation for them to return after their trip to Neshaminy.

Wishing he had been able to speak to Mary alone, Adam promised to stop by on their return trip. He turned and left through the rear door which Polly all too agreeably shut behind him.

Mary abandoned her sewing to watch from the window as Adam and David rode away, then she turned toward the table where Adam's letter lay.

"It's sealed with wax, mistress," Polly said, as if she knew that Mary had planned to read it.

"Most letters are, Polly," Mary said casually. "Put it on Papa's desk with his mail."

Polly picked up the letter and walked toward the window, holding it up to the light. "Looks like parchment. The way it's folded, y' can almost make out a few of the words, though."

"Polly! The very idea, trying to read a letter addressed to someone else—I'm surprised at you."

"Yes, mistress," Polly said, but her half-smile belied her attempt to sound penitent.

Mary watched Polly take Adam's letter across the hall where John Andrews had his office and wished it hadn't been sealed. But her father would soon be home, and he'd tell her what it said. Until then, she'd just have to be patient.

"You didn't tell me how far Neshaminy was," David said a few hours later. Night had fallen, and although the sky was filled with bright stars and there was a bit of a moon to guide them, they couldn't ride very fast. The air had chilled considerably once the sun had gone down, and the buckskin shirt that had seemed so comfortable in the daytime was now inadequate.

"I didn't know it was this far myself," Adam said, although he vaguely recalled that Mary had tried to tell him it wouldn't be an easy hour's journey. *We should have stayed in Philadelphia tonight,* he thought, but knew better than to say so to David.

"And when we get there, will y' know where it is y' are?"

"It's not a large place—everyone will know Ian MacPherson," Adam said with more confidence than he felt.

They rode in silence through several sleeping villages, where packs of dogs came out to give them a noisy greeting, but no humans stirred to see who passed in the night.

"I'm nigh unto fallin' asleep right here in the saddle," David complained after a long while.

"I'm tired too," Adam admitted. "There's a fair-sized barn yonder—it's bound to have a hayrick."

"Then let's try it."

The barn, a sturdy stone building far larger than the modest farmhouse that stood a few hundred feet from it, did indeed have an abundant supply of fragrant hay. Adam and David tethered their horses and soon had spread their blankets over a convenient mound of hay near the door.

"This is better than sleepin' on the floor in Philadelphia," David said, his voice drowsy.

"I suppose so," Adam said. *But at least Mary Andrews had been nearby then.* Adam's last thought before he fell asleep was that he already wanted to see her again.

๛

When Mary awoke the next morning to a cloudy day, her first

thought was of Adam and David. She wondered if they had reached Neshaminy the night before. Mary began each day with prayer, and this day she found herself asking God to care for the two young men and bring them safely back.

"Mornin', mistress." Polly seemed unusually cheerful as she brought in Mary's breakfast tray, and she didn't waste much time in revealing the reason. "The master's back home."

"When did he get here?" Mary asked.

"Late, Thomas said. Master woke him up to care for his horse and said he was tired and didn't want to be bothered this morning, so y'd best wait t' make him read his mail."

"Oh, Polly! If I wasn't so hungry, I'd throw this bun at you," Mary said.

"Throw all y' like, it won't change a thing. Too bad the young men went off like that, so near t' the time they coulda seen Master John—that is, if that's really why they came here."

Mary raised her eyebrows at Polly's words. "What on earth are you suggesting? What other reason would they have for coming here? Just as Ad— Mr. Craighead said, he has a letter of introduction to my father. Like as not, Papa can help him in some way."

"An' if he can't, y' will," Polly supplied. "I give 'em two days at the most before they're back on the doorstone again."

"I hope you're right," Mary said. "And when they do come back, Papa will be here—even if I have to tie him down to keep him from leaving again."

The image brought a brief smile to Polly's usually dour face. "I'd like t' see that—and it might be all that'll keep him here, at that."

"What makes you say so?" Mary asked, sensing that Polly knew more than her fleeting smile indicated.

"Thomas said he wanted the carriage to be made ready for this afternoon."

"Oh, he did, did he? Well, I may have something to say

about that. Let me know as soon as Papa's up, will you?"

"Yes, mistress. Enjoy yer breakfast," Polly added, grinning from the doorway.

❧

Adam and David awoke with the dawn, somewhat stiff from their cold ride the night before, but eager to complete their journey.

"We should tell the farmer that we spent the night here," Adam said. "He might be willing to feed us and our horses for a few coins."

"You'd best go alone," David said. "One look at me and the man might think he's about to be scalped and raise the alarm."

"You don't look at all like a vicious Indian," Adam said.

"Not to y', because you know me. But I saw how that Mary Andrews and her maid looked at me at first. I'm sure they both thought I keep a sharp tomahawk handy t' use on the likes o' them."

There was a bitterness in David's tone that Adam had never heard before. "Even if they thought that at first, they soon knew better. Sometimes we have to give people a chance before we make any judgments about them."

David's sudden laugh startled Adam. "Maybe I was wrong—I'm beginnin' t' think y' might make a pretty fair preacher after all."

"I'm sorry if it sounded like I was preaching," Adam said, embarrassed at the realization that he might have been doing just that. "I'd best go try my skills out on the farmer—watch for my signal—they might just invite us in."

Another hour found Adam and David on the road again, well-fed by the German farmer in whose barn they had slept. In his strange blend of German and English, the farmer had assured them that they were near Neshaminy, and, refusing their coins, had invited them to come back any time.

"That was a nice fellow," David commented as they rode away.

"Yes, he was. Did you notice how he kept pointing to that huge Bible when I tried to give him the money? I think he was trying to tell us that he took us in because of his religion."

"Maybe, but where I come from, it's the thing t' do t' take care o' the stranger amongst us—because we never know when we might need help."

"It was the same way with the Lenni-Lenape in the old days," Adam said. "But times are changing fast—they learned the hard way that not everyone comes in peace."

"The day is too fair for such gloomy talk," David said after a moment. "Want t' see who can get to Neshaminy first?"

"I already know that, cousin—" Adam began, but David spurred his horse, and the race was on.

So they came laughing to Neshaminy, reigning in their horses and arguing good-naturedly about who had arrived first. Adam turned to a middle-aged man who had stopped to watch them and asked his opinion.

"Tell me, sir, which of us reached yonder fence first?"

The man looked from Adam to David and back again before speaking. "Ye shouldna be racing on a public road, lads," he said in a well-modulated voice. "'Tis a danger to all who might chance your way."

Adam felt his face warm at the gentle admonition. "I'm sorry, sir—we didn't think about that."

"We're not very used to real roads," David added.

The man smiled faintly. "That I could tell," he said. "What brings ye to Neshaminy?"

"I'm looking for a minister named MacPherson, Ian MacPherson," Adam said. "Might you be able to direct me to him?"

"I might, considering I am the man ye seek," he said. "That's my house yonder. I was just on my way there after a sick call. And who might ye be?"

Adam dismounted and was surprised to see that Ian

MacPherson was such a tall man. "I'm Adam Craighead, and I'm sorry we had to meet like this, sir," he said. "My father would be very disappointed in me, I'm sure."

MacPherson's hazel eyes searched Adam's, and as a flicker of recognition kindled there, he smiled broadly and reached out to grasp Adam's hand.

"Ye must be Caleb's son—now I can see the resemblance."

"Yes, sir. He asked me to give you his regards—and this." Adam drew the letter from his saddlebag.

"And who might this lad be?" the minister prompted when Adam did not immediately introduce him to David.

"I'm sorry, sir," Adam said again, feeling more awkward and uncouth by the moment. "This is David McKay, my cousin. His father is my mother's brother," he added when MacPherson seemed to be having some trouble making the connection.

"Welcome to ye both," MacPherson said, extending his hand to David. "Come along to the house now—my wife will be glad to give ye breakfast."

"Thank you, but we've already eaten," Adam said.

"Then ye must eat again," MacPherson said. The corners of his eyes crinkled in concert with the smile lines around his mouth, almost the only lines in his fair-skinned face.

This is no dour Scots minister, Adam thought with relief, having pictured Ian MacPherson in a completely different way. "We might just do that, sir," Adam replied.

❧

Mary busied herself about the house as well as she could, trying to pass the time until her father was ready to see her. He had risen not long after she had, but some men arrived soon after, and he remained closeted in his office with them for more than an hour. Then, just as Mary thought she'd have a chance to tell him about Adam Craighead, another group of men arrived, and with a shrug that said "I'm sorry, but I can't help this," John Andrews went back into his office.

"I don't think those men will ever leave," Mary told Polly at lunch time. "Why don't you knock on the door and ask if they care to take lunch?"

Polly looked at her mistress as if she had taken leave of her senses. "Y' know Master John'd have my head if I did such a thing—he's not t' be disturbed when th' door's shut, unless it's really important."

"If you're hungry enough, lunch can certainly be important," Mary said. "Or if the house should burn—"

"Mistress!" Polly said sharply. "I've not heard y' talk so strangely before. Mayhap y' need a dose of spring tonic."

Recalling the evil-smelling and worse-tasting concoction of sulphur and molasses that had been forced down her throat each March in her childhood, Mary made a face. "No, thank you! All I need is some time with my father, and I will have it, one way or another. After this batch of men leaves, I'm going in there, and you must tell anyone who comes to see him that they'll have to wait."

Polly rolled her eyes and was about to speak when they heard the office door open, then the murmur of voices and the sound of the front door closing.

Mary sprang from the table and ran into the hall, where she embraced her father. "So you finally came back!" she exclaimed.

John Andrews looked down at Mary with a puzzled expression. "I must have been gone longer than I thought to get such a welcome. But I know exactly what you want, and this time, you're going to get it."

It was Mary's turn to look puzzled as she drew back and looked at her father.

"What do you mean?"

"I've been preoccupied lately, and we haven't spent much time together. But today I intend to make it up to you."

"I know you can't help it, Papa," Mary began, but he held

up a silencing hand.

"There are many things that can't be helped, true enough—but today we won't talk of that. I have a surprise for you."

Mary laced her fingers and brought them to her chin. "What is it?" she asked, then looking at the amusement in her father's eyes, she thought she knew.

"You brought me a riding horse!" she exclaimed, then threw her arms around him. "Thank you, Papa!"

John Andrews pulled away and shook his head. "No, Mary—that wasn't our bargain."

"Then what—" Mary began, realizing just as her father spoke what it must be.

"Lancaster," he said, smiling with pleasure at the thought that he was making his daughter happy. "I'm taking you to Lancaster this afternoon."

seven

The MacPherson's house was small but comfortable. Adam and David were ushered into the main room, a combination kitchen, dining room, and sitting room, dominated by shelves filled with more books than Adam had ever seen in one place. Ian MacPherson's wife, Nancy, insisted on serving them a hearty breakfast. Although Adam feared that he'd made a poor first impression with Ian MacPherson, he soon found the minister to be a warm man who treated Adam and David as kindly as if they had been his own sons.

"Alas, Adam, in His infinite mercy and wisdom, God dinna see fit to gift Mrs. MacPherson and me wi' bairns of our own," Ian replied when Adam inquired about their family.

"Perhaps 'twas because He knew my husband and I would be needed to take in babes that had none to look after them," Nancy MacPherson said.

"That's right," Ian said proudly. "Thanks to my wife, no young one around Neshaminy has ever been put away in an orphan asylum."

"My parents did the same thing," Adam replied, remembering the succession of frightened children, their parents killed or captured by Indians, that Ann and Caleb Craighead had tended until they could be restored to relatives or homes could be found for them where they would be kindly used.

"Have ye brothers or sisters?" Ian MacPherson asked Adam.

"Only one still living, a sister some fourteen years older. Sarah wed and left home when I was still quite young."

Ian turned his attention to David. "And what of your family, lad?"

"My father traps and hunts half the year. My mother's dead. I have one sister and four brothers, all younger."

"Tell him your brothers' names," Adam urged.

"Matthew, Mark, Luke, and John," David recited.

Ian MacPherson smiled. "Good names, those."

"Everyone calls them the Gospels," Adam said.

"I can see why." Ian turned back to David. "And I ken why ye've left home. There comes a time when every young man has to make his own way. For me, it was in '35. The Lord showed me the way to the American Plantation as clear as if He had me by the hand."

"It must have been hard for you to leave Scotland and go so far away," said Adam, who had begun to miss his wilderness home far more than he had ever thought possible.

"Aye, but I was in the Lord's will, and that made the difference."

There was an awkward silence, then Nancy MacPherson rose and took her bonnet from a peg by the door. "I must look to some chores now—Mr. McKay, will you come along?"

David looked grateful for the opportunity to go outside. "Yes, ma'am. I need to check our horses' hooves. Those Philadelphia cobblestones nigh ruint them."

"Not to mention the damage done from tearin' down the road," Ian said with a faint smile. "We've a fine blacksmith here. Mrs. MacPherson will show ye where to find him."

As soon as the door closed behind them, the minister picked up Adam's letter and broke its wax seal.

"I don't know what my father wrote," Adam said as the minister began to scan the closely-written pages.

Ian MacPherson smiled as he started to read, then his expression grew more sober, until by the time he finished, he seemed moved almost to tears. Adam sat quietly, trying hard not to look at the minister until he refolded the letter and spoke to Adam.

"Forgive me—perhaps I shouldna ha'e read it before ye, but I was eager to know your father's mind. Caleb Craighead is as fine a man of God as I ever met. As I thought might be the case, he's burdened about your future."

"I know that," Adam said, still wondering what his father could have written that would bring tears to his oldest friend's eyes.

The minister stood and walked over to a stand on which a large Bible rested. He opened it and turned to Adam. "Do ye know chapter forty of the book of Isaiah?"

"Yes—my father reads it often. 'Comfort ye, comfort ye my people, saith your God.' Isn't that how it begins?"

Ian MacPherson nodded and continued quoting with his eyes half-shut, not looking at the verses. "'The voice of him that crieth in the wilderness, Prepare ye the way of the Lord, make straight in the desert a highway for our God. Every valley shall be exalted, and every mountain and hill shall be made low: and the crooked shall be made straight, and the rough places plain: And the glory of the Lord shall be revealed, and all flesh shall see it together: for the mouth of the Lord hath spoken it.'"

He turned and looked searchingly at Adam. "Do ye believe those words, lad?"

Adam's mouth felt suddenly dry and his head unaccountably light. *What does this man want from me?* he asked himself, although he knew the answer. "Yes, sir. My father called that chapter his divine orders."

"Orders, indeed," Ian MacPherson said. "When Caleb Craighead came here lookin' for his fare to be redeemed, he testified that God had directed him to leave off schoolteaching and to cross the ocean as a minister of the Gospel. His faith convinced me he was sincere, and I was happy to raise his passage money. Now Caleb asks me to help ye find your vocation."

"Is that what he wrote you?" Adam asked, certain that there must have been something else in the letter to so affect the man.

"That, and some things just between us. I never had a son of my own, Adam, but I ken something of how it maun be. If ye were mine, I'm sure I'd want ye to follow in my footsteps, too. But unless it is a path ye freely choose yourself, the journey will be for naught."

Ian MacPherson's eyes seemed to be looking into Adam's soul, probing to see what kind of person Caleb Craighead's son had turned out to be, and perhaps feeling disappointed at what he found.

"My father thinks I have a vocation for the ministry," Adam said when he could speak again.

"What do ye think?"

Adam looked away from the minister's steady gaze and shook his head. "I cannot say I have had any such call. Anyhow, I know I'm not good enough myself to guide anyone else."

Ian MacPherson shook his head sadly. "Surely ye know the Scriptures better than that. The Lord canna wait for a man to be perfect before He uses him."

Adam remained silent, unable to think of a rebuttal. "My father's a great man and he's helped many people. I know he wishes I'd take up his work with the Indians, but I don't see myself doing that."

"There are many ways to minister, Adam. All must find our own place in the Kingdom. For several of us here in Neshaminy, keeping a school of sorts to train ministers has been our life's work."

"My father mentioned the Log Cabin School," Adam said, relieved for the opportunity to shift the conversation to a less personal level. "Is it still operating?"

Ian MacPherson joined Adam on the settee. "Aye, but the

times ha'e changed. Now young men of a scholarly bent can go over to college in the New Jersey Colony and learn more elevated Greek and Hebrew than we can teach them. At the same time, men of God are in such scarce supply in the wilderness that some near-illiterates undertake to preach with no schooling at all."

"I heard of one such man," Adam said, smiling at the memory of his father's relish in telling the tale. "It seems that he owned a Bible, but had trouble keeping it right side up when he preached from it."

Ian MacPherson nodded. "Aye, until someone told him that the page numbers came at the bottom."

"But then he lost that Bible, and the next one he got had the numbers at the top of the page, and once more people had to tell him he was holding it upside down," Adam said, continuing the story.

"So finally the poor man said right side up and upside down were of Satan, and he'd hear those words no more," Ian MacPherson finished with a flourish.

Adam chuckled. "Do you suppose that really happened?"

"I fear that it certainly could ha'e. At any rate, it makes a good tale."

"Not all tales are equally worthy to tell" Adam said, unconsciously quoting one of his father's favorite expressions.

"Spoken like Caleb Craighead's son, for certain. Well, lad, if ye should ha'e a vocation, ye'll also ha'e our help. Your father tells me ye ha'e studied Latin and a smattering of Greek and Hebrew. Ye could be licensed with very little more schooling."

Adam's gesture took in the book-lined walls. "I'd very much like to read from your library, sir. I thank you for your offer, and I'll consider it."

Ian MacPherson looked disappointed. "'Considering' is a human reaction done with the mind. Ye must seek guidance from the heart."

Adam realized he'd once more revealed his lack of spiritual depth and felt his face warm. "Of course. I know that 'Thy will be done' has to be more than an empty phrase."

"Pray, son, pray as the Bible tells us, without ceasing. Then ye'll ken His will for sure. God always sends signs to those who prayerfully seek them."

Adam nodded. "Yes, sir."

Ian MacPherson stood and smiled down at Adam. "In the meantime Mrs. MacPherson and I would be pleased for ye and your cousin to stay here with us as long as ye have need to."

"It's kind of you to offer, but David and I must return to Philadelphia right away."

As Adam spoke, the door opened and David and Mrs. MacPherson entered.

"The smith says he can shoe our horses first thing tomorrow," David said.

"Then we'll be on our way, with many thanks for your hospitality," Adam said.

Nancy MacPherson looked disappointed. "Oh, dear, I was so hoping that the pair of you would be pupils."

"Not me!" David said with such force that the others laughed.

"We'll have to leave that matter to the Lord, wife. In the meantime, Adam, I'll show ye what ye'd study, should ye decide to come back."

That's unlikely, Adam thought. *Father would love to have the chance to read some of these books, but I'm no scholar.* "Does a man really need to know so much to preach?" Adam said aloud.

"The Word tells us that we must study to show ourselves approved of God." Ian MacPherson looked closely at Adam. "Ha'e ye your own Bible?" he asked.

Adam shook his head. "No. I thought I might find one in

Philadelphia," he added, although he had almost forgotten that his father had urged him to use some of his precious coins to do so.

Ian MacPherson selected a well-worn book from the shelf and handed it to Adam. "This belonged to a friend of mine and your father's who departed this life last month. Before he died, he asked me to give it to someone who needed it. I know he'd be pleased for Caleb Craighead's son to ha'e it."

"I can't accept this—" Adam began, but Ian MacPherson thrust the book into his hands.

"Ye can and ye will, and there's an end to it," he said, and for a moment Adam got a glimpse of another side of Ian MacPherson. He could well imagine the gentle teacher delivering an impassioned sermon that could affect his hearers, perhaps for all eternity. Ministering was a heavy responsibility, all right. That anyone in his right mind would think that Adam could do it was still a mystery to him.

"I thank you, then." Adam took the book and leafed through the pages. "This reminds me of Father's Bible, it's so full of margin notes."

Ian MacPherson nodded. "Read it every day, Adam. Make notes of your own. 'Tis where all our study begins and ends— ye don't need to be a scholar to come to the Scriptures."

As he held the minister's gift, Adam felt strangely warmed. About one thing, at least, he agreed with Ian MacPherson. Whatever his future might hold, the advice and wisdom found in those pages could help him through it.

eight

"Did you hear me, Mary? I said I would take you to Lancaster this afternoon," John Andrews said.

Stunned, Mary looked aghast at her father. "Lancaster? We can't go anywhere today."

It was her father's turn to look as if he doubted Mary's sanity. "What do you mean, we can't go there today? Did you not ask—nay, *beg*—to be taken to Lancaster as soon as I came back home?"

Her father seldom showed anger, but his ruddy cheeks and the set of his mouth marked his displeasure. Mary laid a placating hand on his arm. "Yes, I recall that I did, but that was before—that is, things have changed now."

"And just what has changed so quickly, pray tell? Hetty must have persuaded you to go with her to some frippery—is that it?"

"No, Papa. The general's gala is next week. But while you were gone, you had a caller, and he'll be back in a day or so. You'll miss meeting him if we go to Lancaster."

John Andrews looked puzzled. "I wasn't aware that you'd become my business agent. Just who is this that I mustn't miss seeing?"

Mary's cheeks colored. "He left his letter of introduction. It's there on your desk."

Her father frowned slightly. "I've asked you not to disturb the papers on my desk—" he began, but Mary interrupted him.

"I didn't disturb them, Papa. I just put his letter on top." Mary moved over by her father, who hastily gathered up some papers that had evidently been left by his earlier visitors. She

61

caught a glimpse of a broadside bearing the words "the Sons of Liberty," then found Adam's letter, which had been pushed to one side. "There it is."

John Andrews sank back into his chair as he picked up the letter. "At least you didn't read it for me," he said, and Mary knew she had been forgiven.

She pulled a chair up to the desk and leaned forward in anticipation as he broke the wax seal and began to read. But try as she might to make out the words, she was too far away to tell more than that the letter had been closely written in a fine hand. Foiled at her effort to read the letter Adam had brought, Mary watched her father's face as his eyes moved over the page, rapidly at first, and then more slowly as he re-read it.

Finally he put it down and looked up, gazing vacantly into the distance as if he were seeing some vision. "Ann McKay," he said softly. "After all these years—".

"Ann McKay?" Mary questioned. "The letter is from a woman?"

Once more aware of his daughter, John Andrews looked at her and nodded. "It's from your namesake, as a matter of fact. Just the other day you asked me if she still lived—this letter is proof that she does."

"I don't understand," Mary said, wondering at the effect such a few lines of writing had on her father. "McKay was Adam's cousin's name."

"Cousin? What cousin? What on earth happened here while I was away?"

Taking a deep breath, Mary recounted the events of the past few days. "They went on to Neshaminy, but I told Mr. Craighead to come back when you were here, and he is planning to do so," she concluded.

"You entertained two frontiersmen here alone for two days? What were you thinking? You could have been murdered in your bed!"

"They stayed in the carriage house, and anyway, I knew immediately they weren't the murdering kind," Mary said. "I presume if you knew Mr. Craighead's mother, you must know the family can be trusted. They're some kind of missionaries or something, I think Mr. Craighead said."

"Yes, those men probably are trustworthy, but in the future, you mustn't allow anyone that you don't already know to enter the house whilst I am away. I have good reason for so saying," he added when Mary seemed about to protest.

"All right, Papa. I promise. Now tell me what the letter says."

John Andrews allowed himself a small smile. "'Tis my letter, not yours, but since you've met the young man in question, and I haven't, perhaps you can tell me if he is worth helping."

"Is that what the letter is about?" Mary asked, somehow disappointed.

"That's what letters of introduction are always about," her father said. "'This will introduce you to so-and-so, who is of sterling character and reputation, and so on. Please extend him every courtesy and help him find work, and so on and so on.' This letter isn't much different."

"Adam Craighead didn't say he had come to Philadelphia looking for work," Mary said.

"Then what reason did he give for his sudden appearance on our doorstep? And tell me about this cousin—Ann's letter doesn't mention anyone else."

"You called her Ann McKay—is she Adam's mother?"

"Yes, and she had a brother named Jonathan. I take it that this David must be his son. What business had they in Philadelphia?"

"Apparently they have pelts to sell—I believe David McKay came from North Carolina."

"This letter says that Adam Craighead lives by the

Monongahela."

"Tell me about Adam's mother. How came you to know her, and when?"

Mary's impatience to hear about her namesake seemed to amuse her father. "It was a long time ago. Ann and her brother lived with my parents while their father was looking for a place to settle. Ann cared for my mother, who as you know was something of an invalid."

"And?" Mary prompted when her father stopped talking long before she considered the whole story to have been told.

"And that's all—they lived there for only a few months, then Ann married Caleb Craighead, and I never saw either of them again."

"You know Adam's father, too?" Mary asked.

"Yes. In fact, he—"

"Mr. Andrews!" Thomas ran into the room without knocking, something Mary had never seen him do before. From the look on his face, she knew that something extraordinary had happened.

"What is it, Thomas?" John Andrews stood immediately, braced to take whatever action might be needed.

"I just heard it, sir," Thomas said. "There's been a fight outside of Boston. Th' redcoats went after th' ammunition depot at Concord. Talk is a lot of militia were hurt."

Mary looked at her father's grim expression and felt with him the gravity of the situation.

"What about the British?"

"They were chased back to Boston, sir."

"What does that mean, Papa?" Mary asked, afraid that she already knew.

John Andrews sighed heavily. "I'm not sure, but it could mean we can no longer avoid a fight."

"But Boston—the Massachusetts Colony is far away," she murmured.

"So is England—but apparently not far enough to keep His Majesty from attacking his own." John Andrews turned to the servant. "Let me know if you hear anything else. And Thomas—"

Thomas had turned to go, but stopped. "Yes, sir?"

"I'll still need the carriage this afternoon, but not to go to Lancaster. That trip will have to be postponed."

"You can't leave again so soon—you just got here!" Mary cried.

Her father's expression softened. "I won't be leaving town just yet, never fear. But there are people I must see. And don't worry—as you say, Boston is a long way off, and for the time being, nothing like that is about to happen in Philadelphia."

Mary watched her father leave, her heart heavy. *Nothing will happen here,* he had said, but she knew it was unlikely that any conflict in Massachusetts could long be confined to that colony.

Then another thought made her feel even more forlorn. Adam and David might not need to plan their futures after all. If war came, circumstances would do that for them.

Let Adam come back soon, Mary prayed.

⋅⋅

The blacksmith who tended to Adam's and David's horses turned out to be talkative. He had once hunted around the Monongahela and punctuated his work with a dozen stories of narrow escapes from the Indians. By the time he'd finished his work, the morning was half-gone.

"It'll be too late t' get any goods by the time we get back t' the city," David said when they were once more on their way.

"Remember what McCall told us—you oughtn't buy anything until you're ready to leave, anyway."

"I haven't even got there yet, an' I'm ready to leave right now," David replied. He was silent for a moment, then turned to look at Adam. "Have y' given any more thought to comin' back to Carolina wi' me?"

The question had first been raised at Stone's Crossing, but Adam had avoided giving his cousin a definite answer, unsure as he was of what he might find in Philadelphia. "I want to hear what Mr. Andrews has to say first, but I know you can use some help, and I'd like to see my sister again."

"I wish we could be on our way this very day," David said. "Seems I've been amongst strangers forever."

I know, Adam thought, but he had no desire to leave Philadelphia immediately. "We'll definitely have to spend another night in the city." *I have to see Mary Andrews again,* he could have added.

"If that man Andrews isn't to home yet, I don't intend to stay an' have that Polly girl breathin' down my neck."

Adam laughed. "We'll go there first, but even if Mr. Andrews is back home, we'll find a likely inn."

"Even if Mistress Mary should turn her big brown eyes on y' again?"

"I don't know what makes you say that," Adam said.

"Oh, I think y' do," David said. "Just wait—you'll see I'm right."

❧

John Andrews came home before dark, but before Mary could speak to him alone, several of the men who often called on him came by, and they remained closeted throughout the evening.

I'll talk to him tomorrow, she promised herself as she prepared for bed. Adam and David might come back from Neshaminy the next day, and she intended to make sure that this time they would meet her father.

❧

"Will you tell me what these all-night meetings mean?" Mary asked her father the next morning.

John Andrews looked tired, but not as concerned as he had

appeared to be the day before. "You know everyone who was here last night—we've been doing business since before you were born. The mere threat of fighting will produce a great demand for certain goods, and we want to make sure that they'll be available when our customers have need of them."

"And talking half the night no doubt really helps," Mary said lightly.

"It seems to help you and Hetty when you get together," he returned. "Which reminds me—what is this about her father's party?"

"It's a gala," Mary said. "It'll be General Hawkins' first chance to entertain since they came back from England."

"No doubt it'll be quite an elegant event. I suppose you intend to go?"

"Hetty would never forgive me if I didn't. You're to come, too—she said the calligraphers were nearly finished with the invitations."

He shook his head. "No, thank you. You know I've no stomach for that sort of carrying on."

"But you haven't been to a party in months," Mary reminded him. "I know you always enjoy the music."

"The music is fine—it's the company I'd find offensive. Don't look like that, Mary. You may go if you like."

"Maybe you'll change your mind before then," Mary said, knowing that was unlikely.

"We'll see," he said, dismissing the subject. "You can go to the warehouse with me today if you like—there's a great deal of work to be done."

Ordinarily Mary welcomed the opportunity to go to work with her father. She liked the bustle of the commerce around the docks and enjoyed copying the invoices and bills of lading that would be attached to goods that would make their way throughout the colonies. But today was different.

"I didn't sleep very well last night," Mary said. "Maybe I

should stay here and rest."

John Andrews looked closely at his daughter. "This is about that Craighead man, isn't it? Polly said you seemed to be interested in him."

The color that flooded Mary's face betrayed her and made any denial useless. "They both seem to be worthy young men," she said. "Perhaps you'll have the opportunity to find that out for yourself soon."

"Perhaps. But should they come back, I don't want you to invite them to stay here."

"But, Papa—" Mary began.

"It's my place to do that, should I think it fitting. Send them on to the warehouse if they happen by before I get home."

"Yes, Papa," Mary agreed.

Now all Mary could do was wait—and hope that Adam kept his promise to return.

nine

"Y're goin' t' wear that curtain out, pullin' it aside so much," Polly said to Mary late that afternoon. "Y' don't want company t' know you're anxious about seein' them."

Mary turned from the window, chagrined that Polly had read her so well. "I'm not anxious about anything, Polly. I'm free to look out of my own window as often as I like."

"Yes, mistress, I reckon that's one thing that's not yet been taxed. Should I put an extra joint o' meat in the pot, just in case th' men you're not anxious about should happen t' come back?"

Mary forced herself to sit down and pick up some mending that she'd been half-heartedly working on all day. "I suppose you might as well. Papa might bring home someone for supper—we ought to be prepared, just in case."

"I'd say you was more th'n prepared," Polly mumbled as she left the room.

Mary smiled, not fooled by Polly's grumbling. Despite her words, Mary guessed that Polly also hoped that Adam and David—especially David—would come back soon.

Mary had just gone upstairs to put her mending away when the door knocker sounded. She made herself wait while Polly took her time answering the door, and it was only when Polly called up that someone was there to see her that Mary smoothed her skirts, adjusted her cap, and slowly descended the stairs.

Adam stood in the hallway, even taller and more imposing than Mary remembered. His eyes followed her all the way down the stairs.

"Evening, Mistress Mary," he said. When she held out her hand to him, Adam hesitated a moment. He knew that propriety said his lips could merely hover over the surface of her hand and not touch it, but Adam took the opportunity to firmly kiss Mary's hand, press it afterward, and hold it a second longer than propriety allowed.

"I trust you had a pleasant trip?" Mary asked, her question including David.

"Yes, thank you, ma'am," David said.

"Is Mr. Andrews here?" Adam asked.

"He went to the warehouse—if you like, you may go there to see him, or you're welcome to wait here," Mary said.

"I believe we've heard that story before," Adam said.

Mary hadn't blushed when Adam kissed her hand, but now she did. "He really does want to meet you both. I gave him your letter," she added, answering Adam's unspoken question.

"And? What did he say about it?"

"Only that he knew your mother when she stayed with my grandparents. He seemed to be pleased to hear from her."

"I see," said Adam, who had somehow hoped to hear more.

"We ought to go now," David said.

Mary's eyes pleaded for Adam to stay. "The warehouse isn't far. You could go there in our carriage."

"No, I think not," Adam said, responding to David's violent head-shaking. "We must be on our way. Tell your father I'll come back tomorrow morning."

"But he'll be home soon, I know it." Mary took a step closer to Adam as if her nearness might change his mind.

"Perhaps—but we mustn't stay longer," Adam said.

"Won't you at least have supper with us? Polly put on an extra joint—it's no trouble at all."

At the mention of Polly's name David's face darkened and he gestured toward the door. "Y' promised, Adam," he reminded his cousin.

"Thank you, mistress, but we really must leave."

"We'll see you tomorrow, though?"

Adam looked at Mary, helpless to resist the appeal in her eyes if he'd wanted to. "Yes."

"Until tomorrow, then." Mary opened the front door for them. Even after Adam and David had untied their horses and walked down the street, she stood looking after them.

❧

"I'm beginning to think that this Adam Craighead and his cousin are really phantoms," John Andrews said that evening as he and Mary took their supper together. "Why didn't they come to the warehouse as I suggested?"

"It was late, and since I wasn't allowed to invite them to stay here, I suppose they were concerned about finding somewhere to stay. They said they'd come back tomorrow."

"I hope so," John Andrews said. "I confess I'm curious to see how Ann's son has turned out."

"What was she like?" Mary asked.

Her father's eyes softened. "As a girl, Ann McKay was graceful and gentle, kinder to my mother than my own sister was. Yet she could also be quite forceful if need be."

"Why, Papa! I believe you must have been half in love with her!" Mary exclaimed.

He smiled ruefully. "Half? No, far more than that. I wanted to marry her."

The notion that her father could ever have loved anyone other than her mother was new and faintly disturbing, and it was a moment before Mary spoke again. "Why didn't you marry her, then?"

John Andrews shrugged. "She chose Caleb Craighead—she met him first. But that was all a long time ago."

"Before you met my mother?"

"Oh, yes—and I've never looked back, then or since."

"But you named me after her, didn't you?"

"Yes. I suppose I hoped that you would grow up to be the kind of young lady that Ann McKay was when I first knew her."

"That's quite a tribute," Mary said. "I'd like to meet her."

"Unless you're willing to trek into the wilderness, it's not likely. But apparently you think rather well of her son."

"So will you when you meet him."

"I'll reserve my judgment until then. In the meantime, pass the chutney."

❧

Adam came alone and on foot early the next morning. Intentionally demure in a plain beige morning-gown topped by a half-apron, Mary passed the slow-moving Polly to answer his knock herself. In the shirt she'd mended for him and with his hair pulled back and tied neatly, Adam looked different—but not a whit less like a frontiersman.

"Good morning," Mary returned his greeting. "My father is expecting you," she added formally. She had started toward the office door when it opened and John Andrews emerged.

"You must be Adam Craighead," he said. Extending his hand, he studied his guest.

As Adam had surmised, Mary's father was shorter and less broad-shouldered than he was, but the older man's strength was evident in the firmness of his handshake. Adam nodded. "Aye, sir. 'Tis a pleasure to meet you at last. I was beginning to fear I'd missed the chance."

"So was I. What about your cousin—David McKay, I think Mary called him?"

"He's doing some trading before starting back to North Carolina."

John Andrews turned to Mary. "Ask Polly to brew us a cup of the herbals she found yesterday."

"Yes, sir." Mary hadn't expected to be a party to the conversation between Adam and her father, but taking the tea to them would give her some idea of how they were getting along. *Papa just has to like Adam,* she thought as she went to the kitchen.

"Sit down here," John Andrews invited Adam, indicating a chair. He closed his office door and pulled up a chair opposite Adam instead of taking his usual place behind his desk.

"Thank you, sir." Adam looked around the small, sparsely furnished room. His glance lingered on the jumble of papers covering the desk.

"I read your mother's letter," John Andrews said. "Are you aware of its contents?"

"Yes and no. I didn't read it myself, but Mother told me she asked you to help me if I decided to stay in the city."

John Andrews leaned back in his chair and folded his arms across his chest. "What did she tell you about me?"

His unexpected question caught Adam off guard. "Very little, sir. My mother said you were a good friend to her and my father. She said she hadn't seen you in many years, but she knew you still did business in Philadelphia."

John Andrews nodded. "Did she say anything else about me?"

What else could she have said? Adam wondered. "She told me that you're one of the finest people she's ever known."

A strange look passed over John Andrews' face. "Your mother didn't always have a high opinion of me," he said. He uncrossed his arms and leaned forward, his eyes searching Adam's face. "Your features resemble them both."

Adam felt uncomfortable under the close scrutiny, but he did not shrink from it. *I suppose he needs to satisfy himself about my character,* Adam told himself.

John Andrews finished his inspection and leaned back in his chair. "What would you like for me to do for you, Adam Craighead?"

This time the question was not unexpected, but

unanswerable. "I don't know, sir. Mother thought I might like living in the city, but from what I've seen of it so far, I'm not sure."

John Andrews smiled faintly. "I don't wonder that a lad fresh from the wilderness would think ill of the jumble of people in Philadelphia."

"It's not just all the people here—everything seems to be so unsettled. David and I got in the middle of a brawl the first thing, and now we hear there's been some kind of battle in the Massachusetts Colony."

John Andrews nodded. "Aye, that's true. But Pennsylvania's not like some of the other colonies. Here, the large numbers of Quakers tend to hold down the hotheads on both sides."

"Do you think these disputes with Britain will come to war?"

Before Mr. Andrews could answer, there was a light rap at the door and Mary entered, bearing a tray with tea service and a plate of shortbread.

"Where's Polly?" her father asked.

"She went to market," Mary replied. *And I sent her there,* she could have added, but did not.

Adam watched Mary set the tray down on a small tea table, which she then moved between him and her father. She filled Adam's cup first and handed it to him, along with a dainty square of linen, then repeated the process for her father. "The shortbread is fresh baked. Is there anything else I can get for you, Papa?"

The picture of daughterly sweetness, Mary didn't look at Adam until her father had replied in the negative. Then as she turned away from John Andrews, Mary smiled at Adam in the manner of a fellow conspirator.

"If anyone else asks for me, tell them to wait," her father called out as she closed the door behind her.

"I know your business must occupy a great deal of time," Adam said. "I mustn't keep you from it."

"Nonsense! I always have time for old friends. If you don't stay in Philadelphia, have you some idea of what you might like to do?"

Adam took a sip of the hot tea, which tasted so like the brew his mother had given him for his childhood stomachaches that he almost choked. "Something involving trade, perhaps—moving goods from place to place within the colonies, rather than having to depend on England for it all."

John Andrews looked startled. "Has Mary been talking to you about my business?" he asked, and it was Adam's turn to look surprised.

"No, sir. Why do you ask?"

"Never mind. If you have time, perhaps you'd like to see my warehouse," John Andrews said.

"Yes, I would."

Adam's host rose and made a face as he replaced his cup on the tray. "Dreadful stuff, that—it makes one long for real English tea."

Mary materialized in the hallway as the office door opened. "Are you leaving so soon?" she asked Adam.

"Mr. Craighead is going to the warehouse with me," her father said before Adam had to make a reply.

"I'll get my bonnet," Mary said.

"You aren't invited, Mistress Mary Ann," her father said quickly.

Mary tried to hide her disappointment. "I'll tell Thomas to fetch the carriage."

"No—we'll walk. It's a lovely day and I'm sure Mr. Craighead is quite able to get there on his own power."

"Yes, sir. I'll be glad to stretch my legs."

"Good. And on the way, I want to hear all about your family."

Mary watched helplessly as the pair walked down the street, Adam shortening his stride to match her father's. *I could keep*

up with them, she thought. But that wasn't the reason her
father hadn't wanted her along.

Maybe he's going to offer Adam a job, she hoped, and smiled
at the thought.

ten

Mr. Andrews and Adam had been gone for more than two hours when Hetty came to call, wearing a pale blue gingham dress that accented her eyes to perfection.

"Well, where are they?" she asked, looking around as if she expected Adam and David to emerge from behind the furniture.

"Where are who?" Mary asked, feigning ignorance.

"Why, our frontiersmen, of course. They came back from wherever they went, didn't they?"

"Yes, but I doubt that either would consider themselves 'ours.' Adam Craighead went with Papa to the warehouse. He said David McKay was buying trade goods."

Hetty looked disappointed. "I wish they were here. I want to see their faces when they get this."

Mary saw that the stiff white invitation to the general's gala bore both Adam's and David's names. "What does your father say about inviting frontiersmen to such a formal occasion?"

Hetty took off her bonnet and turned to the smoky gold-framed mirror. She patted her blond curls, then turned back to smile at Mary. "He doesn't know about it, but when he sees what life they bring to the party, I'm sure he'll be delighted."

"You assume a great deal," Mary warned. "Even if they're still in Philadelphia next week, what makes you think they'd consider going to the gala?"

"You and I will have to convince them, of course."

Her friend's words made Mary uneasy, and she shook her head. "I'm not sure it's such a good idea, Hetty. Frontiersmen are the rage in London because they're so rare there. That's

77

not the case in Philadelphia."

"Maybe not, but frontiersmen that look like those two are rare anywhere."

"I'll give the invitation to Adam Craighead, but I don't expect him and his cousin to accept it."

Exasperated, Hetty all but snatched the card from Mary's hand. "I'll give it to him myself, then. He should be back soon—there can't be much to see at a dirty old warehouse." Without waiting to be asked, she swept into the drawing room and settled herself in her favorite chair.

"Are you sure you want to wait? It could be a long time." Mary followed Hetty and sat down beside her, feeling unaccountably annoyed. *I don't want her to be here when Adam comes back,* she acknowledged, then felt ashamed of herself for being so petty.

Hetty's distinctive laugh had always reminded Mary of a scale played on a harpsichord, but today it had a disturbing edge. "I'll wait," she said. "There's nothing I'd rather do at the moment."

"Then tell me about the arrangements for the gala," Mary said, resigned that Hetty had no intention of leaving.

It was well after Hetty and Mary had taken a light lunch that Adam Craighead returned, alone. Hetty stayed in the drawing room while Mary admitted him.

"Where's Papa?" she asked.

"Mr. Andrews had to see to an incoming shipment. He asked me to tell you he'd probably be late again."

"Come in," Mary invited, when Adam seemed determined not to move from the doorway.

"I should be going—" he began, then stopped as Hetty came into the hallway, beaming at him.

"Don't leave yet, Mr. Craighead!" she exclaimed. "I have something for you."

A look of bewildered embarrassment briefly swept over

Adam's face, and Mary cringed inwardly. *He and David would be fish out of water at Hetty's party,* she thought.

"Miss Hawkins, is it?" he said, recovering enough to remember his manners.

"Indeed, Mr. Craighead. I presume you can read?" she added, handing him the invitation.

"Hetty!" Mary exclaimed, but her friend merely laughed again.

"I can read the words, but I don't understand their intention, Miss Hawkins. Why would a British general invite us to his party?"

In response to Adam's expression of genuine puzzlement, Hetty came close enough to put a hand on his arm. "Because I want you to come, and he is my father," she said smoothly. "Please say that you will."

Adam glanced back to the invitation and shook his head. "I'm sorry, Miss Hawkins, but I'm afraid we can't accept your kind invitation."

Good for you! Mary cheered silently.

Hetty dropped her hand and stepped back as if Adam had slapped her. "And, why not, pray? I'm certain you would both find the evening most enjoyable."

"Perhaps we would, Miss Hawkins, but the fact is, we'll be gone from here by then."

Mary looked at Adam in alarm. *Why must you leave so soon?* she wanted to ask, but not in Hetty's presence.

"Surely you can stay a few more days," Hetty said in the honeyed tones she used to get her way with her father. "What must you do that is so urgent that it cannot wait?"

"Several things. For one, my cousin and I must start to Carolina, where he is expected."

Hetty drew her fair brows together in a frown. "A few more days won't make that much difference—you can come to the gala first."

"I'm sorry. We can't," Adam said, perhaps more shortly than he had intended.

Hetty's lips pouted, then curved in a winsome smile. "All right. But should you be delayed or happen to change your mind, the invitation remains open."

"I don't think we will." Adam turned back to Mary, who had been a silent party to the exchange. "I must go now, Mistress. David will fear I've fallen among thieves if I don't get back soon."

Stay longer, Mary's eyes pleaded. "Will you come by before you leave?" she asked aloud.

I want to, Adam's eyes told her. "I doubt it. Thank you again for your kindness to us." Adam turned back to Hetty with a half-bow. "And thank your father for his invitation, Mistress Hawkins. Good day."

"Did you see that bow!" Hetty exclaimed when the door had closed behind Adam. "Oh, what I would give to have that man at the gala!"

❧

Adam walked rapidly back to the inn where he and David were lodging, in part hoping to vent his frustration. He'd wanted to have a more private goodbye with Mary, to tell her—

Adam stopped so suddenly that a boy carrying two loaves of bread almost ran into him. "Sorry," Adam muttered, then walked on, considering what he would have said to Mary if she'd been alone. Her father had seemed to like him and hinted that he might have a job for him, should Adam decide to settle in Philadelphia. Yet there was something strange about the nature of Mr. Andrews' business. On the surface, he imported goods for distribution to other merchants. But Adam sensed that something else was going on, something that possibly involved aid to the Patriots, something that almost surely could be considered treasonable.

Adam had told the peltry merchant that he'd chosen neither

side, yet he knew the time was coming—and that right soon—
when he could be forced to make that decision. Growing up
on a frontier where red-coated soldiers had fought the enemies
that had once stolen him away from his family, Adam had
always proudly considered himself to be a British subject. Yet
in the past few years, the Crown's agents had oppressed colonists with what many regarded as cruel measures.

Who is in the right? Adam asked, knowing there were always two sides to any dispute, but finding no ready answer.
Then he recalled Ian MacPherson's admonition: "God always
sends signs to those who prayerfully seek Him."

Heedless of the people hurrying past him, Adam stopped
and bowed his head. "Please send me a sign, Lord," he said
aloud.

By the time Adam reached the inn, he'd made at least one
decision—he would see Mary Andrews once more before leaving Philadelphia.

"I was beginning t' worry that you'd tangled wi' some mob
or another." David greeted Adam. "Word is that there's fights
breakin' out all over the city."

"I didn't see any today, but down at the docks I met a man
who'd just come from Boston. He said what we heard yesterday about that battle in the Massachusetts Colony was cor-
rect."

"What were y' doin' at the docks? Did y' not get to see th'
Andrews man?"

"I saw him—in fact, I was with him at the time—his warehouse is by the docks."

"Did he offer t' give y' work?" David asked.

"All but. He said he'd been thinking of starting up some
kind of trade with the other colonies. He asked if I wanted to
come in with him on it."

"What did y' tell him?"

"That I'd have to think on it. I told him I was going to

Carolina first."

David had been listening soberly but now he allowed himself a quiet smile. "I was hopin' y' wouldn't change your mind. Fact is, I don't know how I'd get all the goods back wi'out your help."

"You must have made all the trades you were aiming to, then."

"Mostly. I've yet t' see one fellow, then all that's left will be the loadin' up and movin' on."

"There's one more thing that I have to do," Adam said.

"Oh? What's that?"

"I'm going back to the Andrews' house."

David lifted a questioning eyebrow. "Why? Did y' leave something there?"

I suppose that's one way to look at it, Adam thought. "Maybe," he replied.

❧

The streets were dark and vaguely mysterious as Adam made his way to Mary's street a few hours later. He reckoned that the large shipment that had arrived that afternoon would take Mr. Andrews some time to inventory. Therefore, Mary should be home alone.

Unless she went to her friend's house, he thought. Well, he'd do without seeing Mary if it meant also seeing Hetty Hawkins. Something about Mary's friend made him uneasy, something he couldn't quite put a name to.

Let Mary be here, Adam pleaded silently as he reached her doorstep. A faint light gleamed from the drawing room window, but at first there was no response to his knock. After waiting what seemed forever, Adam knocked again.

"I'm comin', give me time," a voice grumbled as the door swung open.

Adam let his breath out in a sigh of relief and smiled. "Good evening, Polly. Is your mistress at home?"

Ignoring his question, Polly peered around Adam. "Are y' alone?"

"Yes. David stayed with the trade goods. Is Mistress Mary here?" he repeated.

"Who is it, Polly?" a now-familiar voice called, and Adam answered for himself.

"Adam Craighead, ma'am. May I come in?"

"Of course—Polly, fetch another candlestick."

Adam followed Mary into the drawing room and stood somewhat awkwardly until she motioned for him to join her on the sofa.

"That will be all, Polly," Mary said when the girl had set the candlestick on the window table.

"I'll be in th' kitchen if y' need me," she muttered as she left.

Adam started to speak and then stopped, unable to form any sensible words.

"Once more I must tell you that Papa isn't back yet," Mary said, her faint smile indicating that she wasn't serious.

Adam nodded. "This time I'm glad. I came to see you."

Mary's eyes shone in the candlelight, which also cast wavering shadows that highlighted her even features. "For what reason?"

She's not going to make this easy, Adam thought. He cleared his throat and made a show of looking down at his hands. "To say goodbye. And to ask you to tell your father that I appreciate his offer. Maybe one day I can accept it."

Mary looked surprised. "Papa offered you work and you're leaving?"

Adam shrugged. "I'd like to stay longer, but I can't. It's a long way to Carolina, and David needs my help."

"I see," said Mary, not sure that she did. "Do you plan to stay on in Carolina, then?"

"I don't know," Adam said. Summoning all his courage, he

looked into her eyes.

Come back soon, they told him. "You'll always find a welcome in this house," Mary said aloud. "Papa said that your parents once meant a great deal to his family."

"Yes. Apparently they knew each other quite well," Adam said. *As I want to know you, Mary.*

"Did you know that I was named for your mother?" Mary asked.

"Not until Mr. Andrews told me."

"I didn't know who Ann was until today, myself."

The other truth they each had learned that day lay between them, unspoken. John Andrews had loved Ann McKay, but she had chosen Caleb Craighead.

"It's getting late—I must go," Adam said after a long moment in which neither spoke.

"Yes—Papa will be home soon."

Adam laughed. "How many times have you said that to me, Mistress Mary?"

"Call me Mary Ann," she said. "I like the 'Ann'—I wish I'd always been known by both names."

"Then good night, Mary Ann."

Adam stood and looked down at Mary, who remained seated and regarded him with pleading eyes. "Do you really have to go? I'd like to hear more about your mother."

Adam hesitated, then sat back down. "My mother isn't big in stature, but she's always been a very strong person. She's always helped my father do his work, and she has the gift of brewing herbs and healing."

"I'd like to meet her some day," Mary said wistfully.

"Come to the Monongahela, then," Adam said. "I'd like you to see our village."

"It's a long way from Philadelphia, isn't it?"

"Many days' journey, although not as far as Carolina."

"What will you do when you get to your cousin's?"

Mary asked.

"I don't know yet," Adam said. "It may sound strange, but—"

He stopped, realizing that perhaps he shouldn't tell her what Ian MacPherson had said.

Mary leaned forward and took one of Adam's hands in hers as if doing so might encourage him to speak. "You can tell me anything," she said earnestly, and Adam believed her.

"I don't yet know what I'm going to do, but I trust God to send me a sign. When He does, if I am to come back here, you'll see me again."

Mary looked puzzled. "How will you find this sign?"

"I don't know. By being ready to recognize it, perhaps."

Tears shone in Mary's eyes. "I pray that God will keep you safe wherever He sends you."

"Oh, Mary—Mary Ann—" Adam picked up the hand she had placed in his and pressed it against his cheek, feeling close to tears himself.

Mary pressed her other hand to his lips. "Hush," she said softly.

Adam dropped her hand and reached for her as she moved forward to come into his arms. Then Mary lifted her head from Adam's shoulder and kissed him, so startling him that it took him a moment to realize what was happening. Once he did, Adam returned her kiss and added a few more of his own, finally cradling her head on his shoulder.

They sat together in sweet silence, bound in a loose embrace, until Polly came stomping noisily into the hall and they moved apart.

Adam sighed. "I really must go this time," he said.

Mary stood, feeling suddenly shy. "Yes, I suppose you must."

"Mistress Merry, do y' need anything?" Polly asked from the hallway.

"No, thank you, Polly," Mary said, surprised that her voice

could sound so normal. "Mr. Craighead is just leaving."

"I should hope so," Polly muttered, just out of his earshot.

"My cousin said to tell you goodbye, Polly," Adam said as he walked to the door.

"The same t' him, I'm sure," Polly said.

With Polly determined to stand watch until Adam had left, goodbyes were brief and formal. But as the door closed behind Adam, his last, long look echoed Mary's own unspoken words.

He'll be back, she thought. With or without a sign, Adam Craighead would be back—she was sure of it.

eleven

April gave way to May, and each day Mary Andrews found herself thinking of Adam Craighead, wondering how far he and David might have traveled that day, and longing to hear from him.

"There's no regular mail service to Carolina," her father told her in response to the carefully casual question Mary posed one day. "However, I deal with a number of bargemen and peddlers who often carry letters along with their goods. Adam Craighead could send something to you by them."

Mary half-smiled, seeing that her father knew exactly what was on her mind. "Would you know where to send a letter to him?" she asked.

John Andrews frowned. "I fear I didn't pay much heed to what he said about where they were going. The McKays live somewhere on the Yadkin River, probably not too far from Salisbury."

"Can you show it to me on a map?" Mary asked.

But when her father had at length uncovered the crudely lettered parchment that his Southern agent had prepared some months earlier, Mary almost wished she hadn't asked. Her finger traced the wavering lines of a stage route from Philadelphia to Baltimore, where a lighter line indicated that the road became cruder. From Fredericksburg, one road led west over the Virginia mountains to Culpeper, then southwest to Orange and Lynch's Ferry, and on to Salem in the North Carolina Colony. Between Salem and Salisbury lay the Yadkin River, near which Adam had said the McKays lived.

"It looks like a long journey," Mary said, overwhelmed at

the knowledge that Adam would be so far away.

Her father looked over her shoulder and pointed out a shorter route. "That's the way packets carry goods from the Delaware River to Norfolk. The water route does away with many tedious overland miles."

"I don't see any roads east from Norfolk," Mary commented.

"No, but by swinging northwest past Williamsburg and on to Richmond, they could pick up the Western Road on to Salem."

"In any case, it looks to be a hard journey," Mary said.

"Five hundred land miles, I judge—but why do you ask? Are you planning to visit the Southern Colonies, by any chance?"

Aware that her father was teasing her, Mary nodded solemnly. "Why not? It'd be a change of air, anyway."

John Andrews rolled up the parchment and put it aside. "If you want that, I'll take you to Lancaster."

"I don't want to go to Lancaster just yet," Mary said quickly. *If I leave Philadelphia, hearing from Adam Craighead will be more difficult,* she thought.

Her father raised an eyebrow in the way he had of showing that he doubted her. "No, but perhaps you should. The way you and Hetty go from one party to another these days must be exhausting."

"Do I look so exhausted?" Mary asked, her smile showing that she was quite aware that she did not.

"No," her father admitted, "but I'll be glad when the hot weather puts an end to most of these frolics."

So will I, in a way, Mary might have said. She had enjoyed the music and the dancing and had been flattered by the attentions of the swarms of British soldiers who all seemed alike. "The weather, or their duties. Hetty tells me that her father is leaving Philadelphia soon."

Mr. Andrews looked interested. "Really? Did she say

where he might go?"

"I'm not sure that she knows—something about raising a regiment of colonials somewhere or another. She didn't seem to be concerned about it," Mary added when her father frowned.

"That young woman isn't concerned about much," he said. "I hope my Mary Ann can keep the good head she has on her shoulders."

"She can certainly try," Mary answered demurely. Her father's use of her middle name reminded Mary afresh of Adam and the miles that separated them.

Her father's expression grew serious. "I haven't said this to you before because I didn't think there was need of it—but you mustn't take too much notice of the young redcoats you meet at these parties."

"I haven't, nor do I intend to," Mary reassured him. *There is someone else on my mind.*

He nodded, seemingly satisfied. "Good. I shan't be here to see you off to the next party, but I trust you will continue to conduct yourself as the Christian your mother and I raised you to be."

"You are going away again?" Mary asked, and he nodded. "I must."

"Then I trust you will conduct yourself as a Christian, too," Mary said solemnly.

"I shall certainly try." He took his daughter's hand. "There's something about Ann McKay—Adam Craighead's mother—that I didn't tell you."

"Oh?" Mary asked. The mere mention of Adam's name made her heart beat faster.

"When I came to Philadelphia in my youth, I was wild and undisciplined. I began to gamble and I soon got into some rather serious trouble. When I thought I had to run away from the law, Ann and her brother went with me. When I asked her to marry me, she told me she'd realized that she wanted the same faith her parents had. She had just accepted Christ into her life, and she urged me to do the same."

Mary could scarcely believe what she was hearing. Her father had always behaved with such absolute decorum and integrity that it was impossible to imagine that he could ever have done otherwise. "So you became a Christian because of Adam's mother?" she prompted when he fell silent.

"Yes, in a way, but it was only when I met Caleb Craighead that I made the commitment to Christ that I've tried to keep since. Caleb thought that Ann and I would marry. After I told him otherwise, he sought her out."

"Is Adam aware of this?" Mary asked.

"I don't know. After he left, it occurred to me that perhaps I should have mentioned it."

"You can tell him when he comes back," Mary said.

John Andrews smiled. "You seem very certain that we'll see him again," he said.

"Yes, Papa, I think Adam Craighead will come back. I just don't know when."

                               ✺

"'Tis no wonder there's no mail service to the North Carolina Colony," Adam said after a particularly rough day's travel had brought them out of Virginia and into North Carolina. "Any news that has to come by this route will be a great deal older by the time it gets there, if it ever does."

David McKay dismounted and unrolled his blanket. "This trail's better than the Great Valley Road," he pointed out. "Besides, a man could use th' coastal packets t' send mail."

"Mayhap we should have used them ourselves—I think Uncle Jonathan had the right idea when he told you to ship the bulky goods by water."

David grinned. "Why, Adam, I'm surprised at you! Looks to me like y' just want t' get this trip done with, 'stead of enjoyin' th' scenery along th' way."

"The country's a right fair sight, and I welcome your company, Cousin. But I keep wondering what's happening back in Philadelphia. Why, we might already be in a war and not even know it."

"I think you're worryin' about somethin' in Philadelphia, all right—an' her name is Mary," David said.

"I do think of her some," Adam admitted. *Whenever I'm awake,* he silently added. Mary was in the last thoughts he had before he slept each night.

"Prob'ly more'n she thinks o' us," David said. "Better get some sleep now—we can make Salem in two more days if th' weather holds."

*

"This seems to be the best attended party of the season," Hetty said to Mary one evening in early June. "Just look at all these people!"

The girls stood at the doorway of the upper floor ballroom of the Massie house, where the last major party of the season was about to get underway. Hetty had saved her best light-weight dress for the occasion, a dark blue satin with ivory lace at the neck and sleeves. Mary's peach-colored gown had seen several parties already, but her addition of a dozen small lace butterflies had given the bodice an entirely new look.

The musicians, garbed in blue silk knee-breeches and wearing powdered wigs, had just mounted a raised platform at one end of the hall and were noisily tuning their instruments. A number of women of all ages had already taken seats along one long side wall. Opposite them, the men stood and waited for the lead-out to begin.

"There aren't as many soldiers here tonight as usual," Mary commented.

Hetty opened her fan and used it as a screen for her remarks about the men who had looked up to nod and bow as they entered. "No men in buckskins, either. How they would liven this sad assembly!"

Mary smiled in spite of herself. "Is it so sad? I see the ensign that was so attentive to you at the Galloway's party—and isn't that the captain you were telling me about?"

As Mary spoke, a tall, blond soldier started toward them. He was about Adam Craighead's height and size, but Mary thought Edward Simmons was a rather pale imitation.

"Good evening, ladies. Now that you are here, the party has begun," he said.

"Captain Simmons, how nice to see you again," Hetty purred as he bent to kiss her hand.

"Thank you, Miss Hawkins." He turned to Mary. "Miss Mary Andrews, I believe?" He held her hand a moment longer than necessary after kissing it, so reminding Mary of Adam that her cheeks colored.

Misreading the cause of her agitation, Edward Simmons smiled smugly. "Will you do me the honor of accompanying me on the lead-out, Mistress Andrews?"

Mary glanced at Hetty, whose mouth betrayed her displeasure. *I can't help it,* Mary signaled with her eyes, but Hetty looked away and fanned rapidly as the ensign finally noticed her and came forward, smiling.

"Of course, Captain Simmons," Mary replied.

From that lead-out, through a dozen quadrilles and minuets and supper afterward, Edward Simmons was never far from Mary's side. Only once during the evening did she and Hetty find themselves seated near enough for conversation, and that with Ensign Nelson Cutter between them.

"Isn't this a marvelous party!" Hetty's eyes glittered, but Mary knew her friend well enough to detect the forced gaiety.

As Mary and the captain took the floor for the next figure, Mary attempted to direct his thoughts toward Hetty. "You must dance with Miss Hawkins. She was so looking forward to seeing you again."

Edward Simmons stared intently at Mary as if he hadn't heard her. He took her hand and silently led her through the intricate figure as if it required all his concentration.

Later, when the party was over and Captain Simmons had accompanied Mary to the street to wait for her carriage, he surprised her by seizing her hand and pressing it to his lips. "May I call on you, Miss Andrews?" he asked.

Taken aback, Mary could think of nothing to say. A flat refusal would be grossly impolite, yet she was reluctant to say anything that he might take as encouragement.

"Forgive me for being so presumptuous, but you must know that I very much want to see you again. May I, Mistress Mary?"

Hetty and the ensign appeared beside them, and Mary knew that Hetty must have heard the captain's question. "Not right away, Captain Simmons." Mary gently disengaged her hand.

"Then when?" he persisted.

"I don't know. I may be leaving the city soon," she added.

"And so may I, Mistress Mary. All the more reason for us not to delay meeting again, don't you agree?"

"Come, Mary, you're holding up the carriages," Hetty said sharply.

Welcoming the interruption, Mary murmured, "Good evening," and accepted Thomas' aid in entering her cabriolet.

Hetty climbed in beside her, and with final salutes from Ensign Cutter and Captain Simmons, the girls were borne away.

"Did you have a good time?" Mary asked when it became obvious that Hetty wouldn't speak first.

"Not as good a time as you, I imagine. What did you do to Captain Simmons to have him eating out of your hand like that?"

"Nothing—and he certainly didn't eat out of my hand," Mary said with some asperity. "He used a plate, same as everyone else."

"Humph! Well, if you decide you don't want him, send him

my way." Although Hetty sounded half-serious, Mary chose to treat her remark as a jest.

"What, and let him join that long line of languishing lovers you've accumulated since you came back from England? Give the poor man a chance."

"That's exactly what I intend to do—give him a chance to break his heart," Hetty said, and Mary welcomed her laughter with relief.

twelve

David and Adam reached the banks of the Yadkin River late on a Thursday afternoon. They saw no one in the vicinity, and David had to call a loud "Hallo!" several times before the ferryman heard them.

"That can't be Joshua Stone," Adam commented as a grizzled old man slowly brought the flat-keeled boat that served as a ferry across the river.

"It's not—that's Moses Murray. Joshua lets him live in th' ferry house in return for runnin' the ferry."

"Well, if it ain't Master Davy McKay!" the old man exclaimed when he was close enough to recognize the young man's face. "The folks hereabout have been wonderin' when you'd git here. Is this your cousin?"

"Aye, Adam Craighead, from the Monongahela."

As they made the return trip across the river, Murray repeated the latest news, asked if David and Adam knew anything more, and seemed to be disappointed when they said they did not.

"The folks was hopin' y'd bring some good news," he said as the raft bumped against the landing. "But news or no, I 'spect they'll be glad t' see y' both."

Although Adam had never before been to North Carolina, and it had been a few years since he had seen his sister, he was made warmly welcome. Within a few minutes of arriving at the sprawl of houses by the river, Adam felt completely at home.

"You haven't changed a bit, Sarah," Adam said to his sister

when she finally let him out of her embrace.

"Ah, Adam, you know 'tis wicked to lie," she said, but her hazel eyes smiled. "I hope you've a mind to stay with us awhile, now that you're here," she added.

"It'll take me some time just to figure out who all these young ones belong to. I had no idea you had such a large family."

Sarah laughed. "They're not all our kin—the entire neighborhood came as soon as they heard you were here. Look at them," Sarah said, waving her hand at the children that had gathered around David. "I'm sure you could tell that those dark-haired and dark-eyed boys are the Gospels, and the girl is their sister, Susannah. The rest of the children in the yard are neighbors—Boones and Bryans and Moores, mostly."

"Who is that?" Adam asked, pointing toward another group that had just come out of the house.

"You don't recognize your own nephews? The taller boy's Prentiss and behind him, that's Isaac. The barefoot girl with the red hair—"

"That's your daughter Hannah," Adam finished for her. "She looks so much like Joshua's mother I'd know her anywhere."

"Yes, her red hair always gives her away," Sarah said.

"You and Joshua have a fine family. I only wish Mother and Father could be here to see them."

At the mention of their parents, Sarah's eyes saddened and she clasped Adam's hand. "Uncle Jonathan tells me that all is not well with them," she said.

"Father had a rough winter, but if Mother's herbals hold out, he should be much better by now."

"I pray that it is so," Sarah said earnestly. "'Tis hard to accept that we might never again meet in this life."

"I know," Adam said. He wished he could think of some comfort to offer his sister.

She straightened and attempted to smile. "Joshua and Uncle Jonathan will be sorry to miss your homecoming."

"Where are they? The ferryman said they'd both gone somewhere."

"They're out in the county after rifles."

"Rifles?" Adam repeated.

"Yes—you must have heard about the fighting in Massachusetts. Thinking that it's coming this way sooner or later, the local militia aims to sign up every able-bodied man who isn't an out-and-out Tory. But there are no weapons to give them."

"I'd think every man around these parts would already be armed," Adam said. "I never yet saw a frontier settlement that lacked for weapons."

"Well, ours does. Most of the men hereabouts do have rifles, but they want to leave them with their women so they can defend themselves if need be. If you and David had just known in time, you could have brought us some from Pennsylvania."

"There are a few weapons in the goods we brought back, but hardly enough to outfit a militia," Adam said.

"And who is this, Missus Stone?" A burly, red-faced man came up to Adam and Sarah. With his hands on his hips, he looked Adam over. "He looks t' be fit for our militia, less'n he's one o' them Loyalist pole-cats."

"This is my brother, Adam Craighead, Mr. McWhorter. He just traveled all the way from Philadelphia with Davy McKay."

The man looked impressed. "Philadelphia City, is it? Well, y' must tell us all that's happenin' there, lad. *Then* we'll see about signin' y' up."

"Not until he's had his supper, at least," Sarah said firmly.

"First thing t'morrow, then," McWhorter said.

The man walked away laughing, but Adam knew he was serious about enlisting him in the militia. If he stayed in

Carolina, he would be called on to help defend it.

❧

As the summer heat began to make Philadelphia almost un-
bearable and the tension between the British and colonists grew
daily, Mary's father continued to disappear for days at a time.
When Mary confronted him and demanded to know what he
was doing, he seemed relieved to tell her.

"We're gathering stores for the Patriots and moving as much
as we can from the warehouse to points outside Philadelphia.
It's slow work and most of it must be done by night."

"If you're caught—" Mary began, but he wouldn't allow
her to finish.

"I don't intend to be."

"Could my friendship with Hetty be putting you in danger?" Mary asked, voicing what she had reluctantly come to
suspect.

"Perhaps you know the answer to that better than I do. Has
Hetty seemed to be curious about what I do?"

"Sometimes, but she hasn't mentioned it lately. In fact, since
the Massie's party, I've seen very little of Hetty."

"That's just as well. I don't wish to interfere with your choice
of friends, but lately I've noticed things about the way that
young lady behaves that I don't care to see you imitate. Perhaps it's good for you both that you'll be apart for a time."

Mary raised questioning eyes to her father. "What do you
mean?"

"As usual, you'll go to Lancaster for July and August. 'Tis
cooler there, and I think perhaps you're ready for the change."

"What about you? Where will you be?"

"I must remain here."

"You'll want Polly and Thomas to stay here, then."

"Yes, but since I've kept on the Lancaster servants, you won't
need them."

"I'll miss Polly," Mary said.

"Well, perhaps you can teach Doris to do your hair—I'm sure she'll be willing enough to learn."

Maybe it's a good thing that Polly will stay in Philadelphia, Mary thought. The girl could be the link between her and Adam Craighead. If Adam should happen to write—or better yet, if he came back to Philadelphia—Polly would see to it that Mary knew about it as soon as possible.

"What do you say?" her father asked when Mary did not immediately reply.

"Yes, I think Doris will make a fine lady's maid. When shall I be ready to go?"

John Andrews seemed relieved that Mary was willing to go to Lancaster. "In about a week, I think. I'll send word by Jenkins so all will be in readiness. And of course you must have time to tell all your admirers that you're leaving."

"Oh, yes, I have so many it will take the better part of a week to write them all," Mary said lightly, but she knew what her father meant. Although General Hawkins had taken away a number of British soldiers, Captain Edward Simmons had stayed behind, and his dogged attentions to Mary had become wearying.

"Perhaps you should call on Miss Hawkins," Mary had told him the first time he had showed up on her doorstep, plumed hat under his arm, his heels clicked together in almost-Prussian precision.

With a look of horror he had shaken his head. "But she's a *general's* daughter," he said, as if that made such a thing impossible.

"The general isn't even in Philadelphia any more—and I know that Hetty would be happy to see you," Mary said, but to no avail.

"I wish you would be happy to see me, too, Miss Andrews,"

he said so earnestly that Mary finally gave up and allowed him a short visit.

Even though she felt uncomfortable with a small social lie, Mary instructed Polly to tell Captain Simmons she was unavailable when he called on her, and she returned all his notes unopened. Still the young officer had persisted, as if each rebuff made him more determined to win her.

"Men are a strange lot, aren't they, Polly?" Mary said one night after a neatly dressed manservant had delivered a nosegay of fringed pinks and white roses "from my Captain, m'lady."

Polly twisted her mouth and shrugged. "I s'pose so, Miss Merry. I sure never heard tell o' a man as determined as that poor Captain Simmons."

"For all the good it does him," Mary said. "Take the flowers away—I don't want them."

"I don't mind havin' their sweet smell in my room, mistress. And that Captain—don't he put you to mind o' that Craighead man, not even a little bit?"

Only from the moment I first saw him, and every time since. It is the only reason I tolerate him at all. Mary could acknowledge the thought to herself, but not even to Polly could she give the words voice.

"There's no comparison between them," Mary said aloud.

"That's the way I thought matters was," Polly said, nodding her head.

"I won't even ask you what you mean by that," Mary said briskly. "There is one thing I want you to do for me after I go to Lancaster."

"Yes, Miss Merry?"

"I don't want Captain Simmons to know where I am. You can tell him I went out of town—that's all he needs to know. But if I should get a letter from Adam Craighead—or anyone else other than the captain—" she added, seeing the look on

Polly's face, "send it on to me as soon as possible. Do you understand?"

Polly grinned. "Yes, mistress. *Very* well."

"Take the flowers and go, then—I'll see you in the morning."

thirteen

"Well, boys, ye made much better time than I thought ye would," Jonathan McKay said when he and Joshua Stone returned a few days later.

"I couldn't get away from Philadelphia soon enough," David said.

"What about you, Adam?" Joshua asked.

"I'm not sure I'd want to live in the city forever, but it was interesting," Adam said.

"Aye, that it is," Jonathan agreed. "I'm glad Davy got t' see it, but I'm not a whit surprised that he won't 'bide there."

"Did y' find any rifles, Pa?" David asked, pointing to the cloth-wrapped bundle strapped to his horse's side.

"Only one or two rusty pieces of no use a-tall. Except for seein' some old friends and meetin' some newcomers, 'twas a wasted trip."

"Time to wash up—supper's laid by," Sarah Stone said, temporarily ending the men's conversation.

Later, as he and Jonathan sat alone, Adam turned the conversation from family news to present circumstances. "What is this rifle business about, Uncle Jonathan? Is there really need for so many arms?"

"Aye, lad, even though th' British aren't yet a-hammerin' at our doorstep an' may never do so, there's many Loyalists hereabouts lookin' for an excuse t' start a fight. Our county committee of safety voted to be loyal to Britain but against taxes imposed anywhere but here. Soon as they heard of the fight in Massachusetts, they passed a resolution that the cause of the town of Boston is the common cause of all colonies. Then they seized all the gunpowder in the county and called for militia volunteers. There's no doubt that they expect a fight."

"So you and Joshua have taken the Patriots' side," Adam said, making it a half-question.

"Aye, that we have, and for a reason, lad. The British never did aught for the McKays when we were in Ireland, and whatever help they claim to ha'e give us against the French we've long since repaid many times over in our taxes."

"Still, isn't it hard to think of yourself as anything but British?"

"I ken what ye say, but they've let us know that colonials don't deserve th' same rights as British citizens. Then there's th' business about holdin' back th' land beyond the mountains—now that the French are gone, there's no reason to keep settlers away from th' Northwest."

"I've heard that some people hereabouts plan to go to the Kentucky land."

Jonathan McKay nodded. "Squire and Daniel Boone are surveyin' it now, after makin' a road o' sorts over the mountains. A few folks will go there. Most won't. We maun be ready to arm the ones that're left."

"You may have to make the rifles yourselves," Adam said. "'Tis not a hard thing to do."

"Aye, I've done some gunsmithing. What's called for is a firelock with a three-quarter inch bore, a barrel eight inches over a yard long, topped by an eighteen-inch bayonet. The ramrod has t' be steel, with the upper end of the upper loop trumpet-mouthed."

"Easy enough, provided you have a stash of the needed materials on hand."

Jonathan shook his head. "Not as such, but most households ha'e odds and ends that can be melted down."

"You can have anything but the cooking pots," said Sarah Stone, who had joined them in time to hear the last part of their conversation. "I refuse to risk the children's vittles preparing for a war that might never come."

"It's already come, Sarah—we just don't know what might be happening in the other colonies," her uncle said. "We must arm a militia—we have no choice."

"Perhaps you could get some rifles over at the coast," Adam suggested.

Jonathan grunted. "The only things you'll find there are Loyalists as thick as fleas on a huntin' dog, and the king's ships takin' Carolina tar and pitch away after unloading rum and molasses—neither of which makes very good gun barrels."

"Then you'll have to make rifles from almost nothing, just like we do in the wilderness."

Jonathan turned to Adam, searching his face. "'Bide here a time and gunsmith for us, Adam. Ye need to get to know your kin."

"I'll have to think about it," Adam said.

"That's not what Father would say," Sarah reminded him, and Adam smiled. Despite the difference in their ages, they had been brought up by the same parents, and Adam well knew what Sarah meant.

"I'll pray about the matter," he corrected.

"Don't be in a hurry to leave us, lad," Jonathan said. "Y'r whole life's yet before ye."

❧

Mary Andrews returned from Lancaster after two months during which she rested far more than she liked. War fever had gripped that town as well as the city of Philadelphia, and all the talk made Mary fear for her father's activities on behalf of the Patriots. She also worried about Adam and David. Neither man had seemed eager to become a soldier, but Mary suspected that both would take the Patriots' side and might, for all she knew, already have signed on with the Carolina militia.

"Miss Merry, it's sure good t' have y' home." Polly's warm greeting reminded Mary of how much she had missed the girl's chatter.

"I'm glad to be back. Has anything interesting happened?"

Polly rolled her eyes and put a fist on her hip. "Now what d' y' mean by that, Miss Merry? I'm sure the master gave y' all the news."

"Papa told me what interested him, but I thought perhaps something else might have happened that he didn't know about."

"Well, Miss Hetty came by a few times to ask when y'd be back—had two different British officers wi' her, like she wanted t' be sure I saw 'em."

"What did they look like?" Mary asked.

"One was sorta red-faced and stout, t'other was some ensign—think y' already met him."

"What about Captain Simmons?" Mary asked, and Polly grinned.

"He did come by some for awhile. Then he finally figgered out you really was gone and not jes' out a-callin'. He wanted t' know where you were, but I tole him it wa'n't none o' his business. I've not seen him since."

"Poor fellow," Mary said, smiling back at Polly. "I imagine he's gotten over his infatuation by now. Is there anything else I should know?"

Polly shook her head. "No, mistress, but Miss Hetty did ask me to tell you she wants t' see you as soon as y' get back."

"Hetty will have to wait—I must wash off this road dust first."

While she bathed, Mary pondered what she ought to do

about Hetty. They had been friends for too long for Mary not to see her at all, yet she realized that continuing their close relationship might be dangerous for her father.

Then there was the matter of being friendly with the British soldiers. Most that Mary had met seemed to be decent young men who had generally been posted to the colonies unwillingly. But when—or if—fighting broke out between the British and the Patriots, they would be her enemies. It would be better for Mary to avoid the British soldiers altogether—but to do so might also invite suspicion and thus endanger her father.

I wish Hetty had just stayed in England, Mary sighed. Her life would certainly have been simpler.

❧

Summer came in lush beauty to the land around the Yadkin River. Adam fished with Davy and the Gospels and also got to know his nephews, Prentiss and Isaac, who plied him with questions about his life among the Lenni-Lenape. David's sister, Susannah, was fascinated with the bracelet Adam wore and asked him to try to get someone to make her one like it.

"I can do better than that," Adam said and handed it to her. He'd been wearing it from habit since the day he'd first seen Mary Andrews. Anyway, Karendouah was miles away and Adam had long ago dismissed her from his thoughts.

The bracelet was too large for Susannah's slender wrist, so Adam showed her how to separate the strands and re-tie them. Soon even the Gospels were cutting strips of leather and plaiting them Indian fashion. Adam stayed busy making and mending rifles whenever he could get the materials, and with Jonathan and Davy he ranged far into the countryside. Sometimes they watched the militia drill to the somewhat ragged accompaniment of a drum and fiddle, but as neither planned to stay in Carolina permanently, Adam and David didn't join it.

At his sister's urging, Adam began to go with her to visit the sick and read to them from his Bible.

"The people hereabouts have no one to minister to them, and they're hungry for the Word."

"I'm not a minister," Adam reminded her.

"No, but you can read the Scriptures to them and pray for them. The healing of the body always goes better when the spirit is calm."

Although awkward and self-conscious at first, Adam soon realized that what he read or prayed was not as important as the fact that he represented a link between God and those his sister sought to help. Adam had no trouble praying sincerely for their healing, but his private devotions were quite a different matter.

Recalling the advice that Ian MacPherson had given him, Adam tried to pray earnestly. Yet he felt no sense that God heard him, much less that He would give him a sign to direct his life. With each passing day, Adam felt more restless and less certain of what he was meant to do.

On the other hand, his cousin Davy knew exactly what course he wanted his life to take. One day as he and Adam fished by themselves in Dutchman's Creek, Davy told his cousin his decision.

"Next trip that Dan'l and Squire Boone make to the Kaintuck, I'm goin' with 'em."

"What does Uncle Jonathan have to say about that?" Adam asked.

"I haven't told him yet, but he shouldn't be surprised. Pa knows I've been a-wantin' to go over there."

"He'll miss trapping with you come October."

Davy shrugged. "The Gospels'll be old enough soon, and anyways, Pa's got other things on his mind these days. Why don't y' go with me, Adam? They say that th' land o' milk an' honey's got nothin' on Kaintuck."

"Yes, but from what I've heard, it's also a vicious land. The Indians—"

David made a derisive sound and shook his head. "Y' need say n' more—I see that you lack the stomach for pioneerin'."

"It's all I've ever known, Davy," Adam said, seeking to mollify his cousin. "If I'd wanted to keep pioneering, I'd have stayed where I was."

"'Tis not th' same," Davy insisted. "There's no land left in Pennsylvania any more. If y' heard the Boones talk about the Kaintuck, y'd want to come, too."

Adam shook his head. "It's not for me, but if pioneerin' is your heart's desire, then I wish you Godspeed. I just wish that I could be as certain about what I want to do as you are."

David's declaration made Adam more restless. Although he'd written his parents that he'd probably stay in Carolina through the winter and make some decision about his future in the spring, Adam didn't want to wait that long. *Send me a sign,* he had prayed, but none had come.

Well, Adam thought as he walked alone on a high, remote ridge early one morning, *If God chooses not to send a sign, I suppose I'll just have to do the best I can on my own.*

At that moment, Adam heard a strange, almost human cry. At first he thought one of the valley sheep had strayed into the hills and become snared in the underbrush, then he realized that the sound seemed to be coming from the sky. Adam climbed onto a rock outcropping near the top of the hill to gain a better view. What he saw all but took his breath away.

A bald eagle soared in the sky above the treetops, gliding from side to side as its keen eye scanned the ground beneath its powerful wings. Without warning, it suddenly plummeted to the earth, and Adam's first thought was that an unseen Indian must have brought it down with a well-placed arrow.

But then the bird reappeared, having captured its prey, and a few flaps of its wings brought it to a tree atop an adjoining hill. Fascinated, Adam crouched on the rock and watched. Although he was too far away to make out the details of the scene, the eagle seemed to be feeding its young. It soon left the nest behind, however, and once more split the sky with its wedge-shaped wings.

Adam had seen eagles before, of course, but never had he been so close to one. Never had he been able to see how beautiful its strength was, how powerful, yet graceful it was as it sailed in the air. *God did well when He made you*, Adam thought, making it a prayer of praise. He was aware of a strange warmth, much as he had felt when as a child he had surrendered his life to Jesus.

Reminded of the words that Ian MacPherson had quoted, Adam spoke them aloud. "'They that wait upon the Lord shall renew their strength; they shall mount up with wings as eagles; they shall run and not be weary; they shall walk, and not faint.'"

Adam dropped to his knees on the flinty surface of the rock and clasped his hands together in desperate supplication. *Lord, I've tried to wait on You, I really have*, he prayed. *I want to do Your will, but I don't know where to go or what to do. If You want me to leave this place, send me a sign, Lord, and I'll do my best to understand it.*

Adam opened his eyes and let out his breath in a ragged sigh. His prayer might lack the eloquence of his father's, but it had been as sincere. Adam stood and shaded his eyes with his hand as he scanned the skies in search of the eagle. Nothing appeared.

It must have seen me, Adam thought. Fearless as eagles were, they avoided people, and one feeding eaglets would be doubly wary. Disappointed, Adam bent to pick up his rifle.

Suddenly, the air resounded with the eagle's distinctive cry, and Adam looked up in time to see not one, but two eagles soaring high overhead. They flapped their wings, then glided, climbing higher and higher as they flew to the northeast.

Adam watched them fade into specks, then disappear altogether. He stayed where he was a long time in hopes that they might return, but he knew he had seen the last of them.

fourteen

That evening when Adam told Sarah and Joshua what he had seen, they looked clearly puzzled.

"There's not ever been an eagle in these parts that I know about," Sarah said. "Uncle Jonathan claims our ridges aren't high or lonely enough to suit them."

"And you say there were eaglets in the nest?" Joshua asked. "This isn't their usual nesting time."

"Maybe you saw a goshawk," Sarah said. "Some of them are almost as large as eagles."

I know what I saw, Adam thought, but he knew it was useless to argue the point. "Maybe," he said. "Anyway, whatever it was reminded me that it's time I was moving on, myself."

"Not so soon!" Sarah cried. "I thought you'd stay with us through the winter, at least."

Joshua looked concerned. "Early fall storms can be hard on travelers in these parts. If you plan to go home, you'd best not wait."

Adam nodded. "I agree, and I intend to leave immediately. But I'm not going home just yet."

Sarah looked at her younger brother knowingly. "I think I can guess where you're going—and for what reason."

Joshua looked at his wife in surprise. "What's this?"

"Davy must have been talking out of turn," Adam said.

"Not only Davy, Adam. Do you have any idea how often you've spoken about Mary Andrews and her father?"

Adam's face reddened, bringing smiles to the others. "John Andrews did offer me work in his business," he said, but Adam knew that as far as his family was concerned, his return to

111

Philadelphia was the decision of a lovesick youth.

Later, when they were alone, Sarah brought up the subject of Mary Andrews. "I hope she'll be a worthy helpmeet to you," she said. "Should you decide on the ministry, you'll need such a woman."

"She might have something to say about that," Adam said. "Anyway, I have heard no such call."

His sister laid the palm of her hand against Adam's cheek and smiled faintly. "I wonder if you've really been listening. Perhaps it was no accident that you saw two eagles."

"Do you think it could have been a sign?"

"I don't know, Adam—but I believe the Lord is dealing with you. Whatever else you do, you must take time to listen to Him."

"I'll try," Adam promised.

The next day, Adam waved a last goodbye from the ferry, then turned northeast, the direction the eagles had taken. However he might interpret their flight, Adam thought his sister was right about one thing. It was no accident that there had been two of them.

&

"Miss Merry! Wake up!"

Polly's frantic voice brought Mary instantly awake. "What is it? What's the matter?"

Polly stood by her bed, a candlestick illuminating the fear in her face. "Get dressed and go out the back door," Polly said. "Hurry!"

Mary pulled a petticoat over her head, then struggled into a cotton day gown. "Where are we going, and why?" she asked as Polly thrust Mary's shoes and stockings into her arms.

"Never mind. Just *go*." To punctuate her words, Polly pushed Mary toward the door.

When she reached the staircase, Mary began to understand Polly's urgency. From the doorstep came angry voices calling for John Andrews to come to the door.

"Open it or we'll break it down!" someone called, as another apparently began kicking at the door.

Mary needed no further urging to quit the premises in haste. At the kitchen door Polly stopped and motioned for Mary to wait while she opened the door a cautious crack.

"They don't seem t' ha' thought o' guardin' th' back door," Polly whispered. "Run for the carriage house."

Still barefoot, Mary did as she was told. Inside, Thomas waited with the cabriolet. As soon as Polly and Mary were seated, he walked the horse down the alley until he was a safe distance away from the house, then maneuvered onto the street and whipped the horse to a trot.

"That was close," Polly said when it was apparent that they were going to make good their escape.

"Who were those men?" Mary asked, although she had a pretty good idea. Several threatening letters had lately been delivered to the house, warning John Andrews to "mend his ways" and "mind who you trade with."

"They were a mob, mistress," Polly said darkly. "One man alone at first, an' when I said th' master wasn't to home, he didn't believe me. 'We'll see about that,' he says, an' the nex' thing I know, there's a ha' dozen about, bangin' on th' door and demandin' t' be let in. I don't see how y' could sleep through all that din."

"I was dreaming of a storm," Mary said, not adding that in the dream, she and Adam had been running through an open field beneath menacing clouds, accompanied by loud peals of thunder. "What will they do to the house?"

"Nothin', I hope," Polly said, but both she and Mary knew their dwelling was likely not to escape the mob's wrath.

"Anyway, I'm glad Papa wasn't home," Mary said.

Reaching the docks, Thomas stopped the carriage and slid down from the driver's seat. "I'm just goin' to check the warehouse an' see if Master John's there," he said. He tried to speak reassuringly, but Mary could hear the undercurrent of fright in his voice.

"Hurry—I don't care to be left alone on the docks in the dead of night."

"The docks 're prob'ly safer in the night than the day," Polly muttered.

She and Mary watched Thomas walk rapidly toward the dark bulk of Andrews Import Company.

"As soon as those men find that Papa isn't at home, they'll probably make straight for the warehouse," Mary predicted.

"Thomas'll be back t' us by then," Polly said with more hope than conviction.

Mary buckled her shoes and climbed down from the carriage.

"What are y' doin', Miss Merry?" Polly sounded half-alarmed, half-annoyed, and Mary laughed.

"What else would I be doing on such a fine night as this? We're going to take a little carriage ride."

"Miss Merry, have y' lost y'r mind altogether?"

Without bothering to answer, Mary climbed up to the driver's seat and gathered the reins, prepared to come to Thomas' rescue if necessary. After what seemed to be an eternity, she saw him coming back to the carriage. But before she could express her relief that he was all right, Mary saw that he was being followed by several shouting men.

Quickly she slapped the reins and maneuvered the carriage so that Thomas could vault onto the seat. Mary wielded the carriage whip to keep the other men from attempting to do the same.

"Drive!" Mary cried, but Thomas, rapidly leaving the shouting men behind, needed no encouragement.

"What was that all about?" Mary asked when Thomas finally slowed the cabriolet and they had a chance to catch their breath.

"I dunno, mistress. Those men weren't the reg'lar night

guards. I couldn't make out any faces, but they was wearing some kind o' ribbon in their vests, best as I could tell."

"That doesn't make sense," Mary said. "The Sons of Liberty sometimes wore a ribbon rosette as a sign of their allegiance, but there would be no reason for them to chase away Thomas, whom they all know on sight."

"The men what came to th' door earlier had such ribbons," said Polly, who had leaned halfway out of the carriage so she could hear the conversation.

Thomas brought the vehicle to a stop near a streetlamp on a quiet side street. In its faint light Mary could see the concern that etched his face.

"Are y' sure, Polly?" he asked sharply, and she nodded.

"I'd stake m' life on it," she said.

"There'd be no reason for the Sons of Liberty to harm Papa, would there?" Mary asked.

"Of course not. But I'm wonderin'—"

Although Thomas didn't finish his sentence, Mary knew what he could have said. *Maybe those men weren't Sons of Liberty at all. Maybe they were Loyalists merely pretending to be Patriots.*

Mary shivered and hugged her forearms as if she were chilled. "Thomas, Polly and I will wait here while you walk back to the house and see what's happening. If the men are gone, we'll return home."

"Yes, mistress. The two o' y' watch out, now," he said before he disappeared into the night.

Polly and Mary waited in silence. A long time passed before Thomas returned.

"Well?" Polly asked, but one look at Thomas' face in the faint glow of the streetlamp told Mary more than she wanted to know.

"Y' can't go back there, Mistress Mary. The house is all afire."

fifteen

Traveling alone and in a welcome spell of dry weather, Adam made the return trip to Philadelphia in less time than he and David had covered the same distance. On his best day he made about sixty miles, but out of consideration for his horse, he usually traveled fifty or so. He slept on the ground a safe distance from the road, with his rifle cradled in his arm and his horse hobbled nearby.

In every town, the possibility of war and its effects were openly and often loudly discussed. Adam rode from Lynch's Ferry to Culpeper with a peddler who complained that no one was buying imported goods any more. "I'd be tarred an' feathered if I offered t' sell so much as a paper o' pins from over the ocean," he said.

"You must be having a hard time making a living," Adam said.

"Aye, but I'd rather starve than fatten the British merchants. I've found a few sources o' local goods, and these are all my store now."

Immediately Adam was reminded of Mary's father. "I know a Philadelphia merchant who started looking for such goods some months back."

"Aye? He should soon be a wealthy man, then. I hear tell many of the ladies of quality in th' East have taken t' wearin' homespun along wi' their servants, and their menfolk won't cross them."

"Maybe it's just a passing fancy," Adam said, while acknowledging to himself that it might be one more indication that the colonies were heading for a dramatic showdown with their parent country.

"And mebbe you'll swap your buckskins for osanburg," the peddler said, eyeing Adam's clothing with interest. "Osanburg's what y' need t' be a-wearin' in the city."

"No, thanks," Adam said.

"I'll give y' a buck for th' pants, then, and throw in the osanburgs for free. City ladies are right fond o' osanburg."

"Maybe, but my lady in Philadelphia likes my buckskins," Adam said.

The peddler grinned and touched his hand to his forehead in a rough salute. "Then gi' my greetin' to your lady, and luck t' yourself, sir."

As the man rode away, Adam's smile faded. The closer he got to Philadelphia and to the possibility of seeing Mary again, the more unsure of himself he felt. He truly believed that his future was somehow bound with hers and that whatever he did, he wanted her by his side. However, Adam wasn't sure that Mary felt the same way. Her father, who had welcomed Adam as the son of old friends, might feel quite differently about having a poor frontiersman as a son-in-law.

Worst of all, perhaps he hadn't received any sign at all, but had merely allowed his desire to see Mary Andrews overrule his judgment. When Adam got to Philadelphia, what would he find?

"Take therefore no thought for the morrow: for the morrow shall take thought for the things of itself. Sufficient unto the day is the evil thereof."

The passage came into Adam's mind unbidden and reminded him of the many times he'd heard his parents quote it.

Whatever awaited in Philadelphia, Adam prayed for the strength to face it.

❦

"Miss Merry? Wake up."

Mary's eyes flew open, and for a horrible moment she felt a

formless fear as she realized she wasn't in her familiar bed. She rubbed her eyes and looked around. "What is it?" she asked groggily.

"I'm sorry if I gave y' a start—y' was dozin' so peaceful I hated to disturb y', after not sleepin' any last night. But we're here, mistress—back in Lancaster, where y'll be safe."

"Is Papa here?" Mary asked the servant who came out to meet them.

Doris shook her head. "No, Mistress Mary, an' we wasn't expectin' you, either. But come in, child, y' look all done in."

"She is," Polly said, and told Doris what had happened to the Andrews' town house.

"How terrible!" she exclaimed. "But don't worry none about your Master Andrews—I'm sure he'll come lookin' for you here straightaway."

Mary felt a stab of fear as she realized that Lancaster was the first place that anyone would look for her father, and therefore the last place he should be.

"Thomas, as soon as you've rested, you must go back to Philadelphia and find Papa. Warn him he mustn't come here."

"But Miss Merry—" Polly began, but Mary interrupted her.

"Whoever burned our house and took over the warehouse can mean only harm to Papa."

"I think he already knows that, mistress," Thomas said gently. "Master Andrews is able to take care of himself, all right."

"Then at least let him know that I'm safely here," Mary said.

Thomas nodded. "I will, mistress."

"Come on to bed wi' y' now," Polly said, leading Mary by the hand to the room where she always stayed when she was in Lancaster. "Y're too tired t' think straight. Things'll seem much better after a good sleep."

❦

The last few miles between Wilmington and Philadelphia

seemed to last forever, yet as Adam neared the city, he made himself stop at an inn. He stuck his head under the courtyard pump, then stripped off his shirt and washed his upper body. His chest scar throbbed and felt tight, as it sometimes did before a change in the weather. Yet the setting sun was surrounded by red clouds, an omen that usually indicated fair weather.

A big storm's coming soon, Adam told himself. But rain or shine, he'd soon see Mary. Thinking of their meeting, Adam hoped that she'd answer the door herself, but even if she didn't, he'd know by the look on her face how things stood between them. Perhaps it would be another sign to guide him on his way, another indication of whether God had led him to Mary Andrews for a purpose.

The next morning dawned fair, but a few clouds had begun to gather in the west as Adam led his horse through the crowded streets of Philadelphia. He forced himself to slow down as he turned the corner into Mary's street. Eagerly Adam's eyes turned toward the familiar green door and white-curtained windows that marked the Andrews house. What he saw brought him to an abrupt halt.

Adam gaped in disbelief at the blackened hull that had been Mary's home. The adjacent houses had been less damaged, but appeared to be vacant.

"What happened here?" Adam asked a stocky leather-aproned workman who was planing lumber in front of the house on the right.

The man glanced with disdain at Adam's buckskins. "Are y' from so far in the woods that y' can't tell when a house has burnt?"

"Aye, I see that well enough," Adam said mildly. "Might you know if the people escaped harm?"

The workman shrugged. "I suppose so, since 'tis said that no one was t' home at the time. Mr. Franklin's fire brigade kept the fire from takin' these dwellin's, but as y' can see, they're still a fair mess."

"Do you know where the people who lived here are now?"

The workman turned the plank and ran his hand across its surface before he replied. "I don't get paid t' answer questions."

"If I give you a coin—" Adam began, but the man's gesture stopped him.

"Give me what y' like, I can't tell y' what I don't know. If the folk who lived here are still in the city, I've not seen 'em."

Adam looked at the ashes that had been Mary's elegant home and felt almost physically ill. "How long ago was the fire?"

"A couple of weeks, more or less. I been workin' here less 'n a week, myself."

Adam thanked the workman and walked to the end of the block, then up the alley behind the houses. The back wall still stood, looking almost untouched except for the heavy black soot that streaked the empty windows and the rear door. The carriage house hadn't burned, but the upstairs window had been broken out, and it was evident that the now-empty building had been looted.

Adam's horse lowered his head and nickered, seeing the pile of hay that still stood in the carriage horse's stall. "No time for that now," Adam murmured.

Quickly Adam made his way toward John Andrews' warehouse, his mind churning with fears and unanswered questions. Even if John Andrews himself wasn't there, someone was bound to know if he and Mary were safe and where he could find them. Just knowing that much would help relieve his mind, though Adam knew he wouldn't rest until he could see Mary and assure himself that she was all right.

The strong scent of the sea told Adam that he was near his goal, and he quickened his pace. The streets had become more congested, and he dismounted to thread his way through the carriages, peddlers, and draymen thronging the docks. Adam was almost in front of the warehouse before he saw it—or rather, saw where it should have been. A pile of ashes and jumbled, blackened debris was all that remained.

Mary's house didn't burn by accident, and neither did the warehouse, Adam thought. It was one thing for a home to burn, perhaps through careless neglect of a candle or lamp, but it was too much of a coincidence that the same family's business would also be destroyed accidentally.

Dazed, Adam stared at the ruins for several moments. Then he turned and made his way across the street to a tavern.

It was not yet lunchtime, and only a few customers sat around the tables as Adam approached a serving woman and asked what had happened to the warehouse.

"It burned in th' night a couple weeks ago," she said matter-of-factly. "Can I fetch y' a tankard?"

Adam shook his head. "No, thank you. Do you know Mr. Andrews—the man who owned that building?"

The woman shook her head and turned to leave.

"Wait—is there someone else here that might know what happened?" Adam asked quickly.

Fear touched the woman's face, and again she shook her head. "You'd best leave," she said in a low voice. "We know nothin'."

Adam went back outside, pondering what to do next. He was almost certain that the serving woman knew John Andrews and could have told why the warehouse had been burned, but fear kept her from any discussion about it.

Fear of what? he wondered. John Andrews hadn't openly discussed politics with Adam, but there was no doubt in Adam's mind that Mary's father supported the Patriots.

If the British authorities had found out about it, they would have arrested the man and perhaps confiscated his property, but it would make no sense for them to burn it. On the other hand, a group of Loyalists might act unofficially, with the

British looking the other way, to take care of quickly by mob rule what would take the courts months to consider.

"Pardon me, sir, but I heard what y' asked in yonder."

Adam turned to look at the old man who had come up to address him. "Do you know anything about the warehouse fire? I particularly want to know if the Andrews family is all right."

"We canna talk here on the street. Follow behind me, a few steps back."

Can I trust this stranger? Adam wondered. But if he wanted any information about Mary, he had no choice but to comply.

sixteen

Adam untied his horse and did as the man had directed. He walked a block away from the docks, then turned north and entered a narrow lane where the dwellings were considerably smaller than those on Mary's street. The old man stopped in front of a ramshackle livery stable.

"Leave yer horse here," he directed.

"But—"

"It's all right," he said gruffly. "Tie it yonder—no one will steal it."

"I hope not," Adam said.

"Not from the city, are y'?" the old man said when he had ushered Adam into stuffy quarters uncomfortably close to the stable.

"No, I'm not. Now will you please tell me what happened to the Andrews?"

"First y' must tell me your connection wi' them."

"John Andrews and my parents were friends years ago. I met him and his daughter a few months ago. He told me I could help him in his warehouse if I decided to stay in Philadelphia."

"Well, that's unlikely now, I'd say. Far as I know, nobody was hurt in the fires. You knew the house was a-burnt, too?"

Adam nodded. "I went there first."

The man's eyes narrowed shrewdly. "Mistress Mary is a pretty little thing, at that. Well, the house and warehouse both went up on th' same night, an' no one's seen either father or daughter since, that I know of."

"Who did it?" Adam asked. "Those buildings didn't burn

by accident."

"That's a question y' don't want t' ask around here," the old man said. "No one knows fer sure, but they say that the men that torched them wore Sons of Liberty ribbons."

"You mean they were Patriots?" Adam asked, incredulous.

The old man shrugged. "All I'm tellin' y' is that someone's out t' get John Andrews fer some reason y' don't have any business knowin'. If y' take my advice, y'll go back t' where y' came from and forgit that y' ever knew anybody by that name."

"You really don't know where they are?" Adam said. "I mean them no harm."

The old man smiled mirthlessly, showing gaps where he had lost several teeth. "I'm sure y' don't, 'specially where Mistress Mary is concerned. But even askin' questions about 'em could bring y' to harm."

"Surely you overstate the case," Adam said.

The old man rose and motioned for Adam to leave. "No. I've had my say, an' if you've half th' wits t' match yer looks, y'll do as I say."

Adam retrieved his horse and started back toward the docks, wondering what he should do next. One thing was certain—he couldn't take the man's advice. He didn't know how he was going to be able to do it, but he had to find Mary.

Dark clouds had covered the sun and a stiff breeze began to blow. The storm Adam had anticipated was about to break. *Show me what I should do, Lord,* he prayed as once again he stood before the ruined warehouse.

You must go to Neshaminy.

The thought came into Adam's mind almost in the form of an order, and suddenly Adam felt a sense of relief. Of course that was what he should do. With his connections with so many people in Philadelphia, Ian MacPherson could help him. Mounting his horse, Adam turned and headed out of the city.

*

"Are you alone, son?" was Ian MacPherson's only question when Adam arrived, wet and bedraggled, at his doorstep.

"Yes, sir. David McKay stayed on in Carolina."

"Come inside and get out of those wet clothes," his wife ordered. "You look like a drowned rat."

After he'd changed his clothes and had supper, Adam briefly told Ian MacPherson what had happened since they had parted. "So now I need your help," he finished.

"I'd hoped ye'd come to say ye were ready t' pursue the ministry, but of course I'll do what I can t' help ye find your friends. I know John Andrews t' be an upright man."

"I feel that I was led to come back to Philadelphia, although I still don't know why. Perhaps I was meant to help them."

"We'll pray about it, then ye must get some rest. In the morning we'll speak of what ye can do," Ian MacPherson replied.

*

Barely a week after she had left Philadelphia for Lancaster, Mary was on her way back to it. The jolting discomfort of the cabriolet, which hadn't been designed for long distance travel, mirrored her life since the fateful night her house had been burned.

"We'd make better time riding double on the carriage horse," Mary said as the cabriolet stopped again, this time when a Conestoga wagon in front of them lost its wheel and blocked the way.

"I b'lieve y're in some hurry t' get back t' the city," Polly said.

"I'm tired of being idle. I ought to be helping Papa any way I can," she said.

"I'm still not so sure th' city's safe for the either of y'."

"Whoever burned us out didn't want to harm us—they'd not have made so much racket before setting the fire. They meant to warn Papa. I don't believe we're in any danger."

"I hope you're right, Miss Merry," Polly said without much conviction. "I'd like nothin' more than t' think that things'll get back t' th' way they was."

"So they will, Polly, but it'll take time."

Mary spoke confidently, but in her heart she knew that their lives could never be the same. She recalled how her relief at knowing that her father was safe had been tempered by the realization that his livelihood had been lost along with their home. "What will we do now? How will we live?" Mary had asked him.

John Andrews pillowed Mary's head on his shoulder and spoke quietly of his trust that God would provide for them. "I've already found a place for us to stay, and I still have work to do. We'll be all right."

"But don't you still fear the men that did this to us?"

John drew back and looked into his daughter's eyes. "Not as much as I fear letting those cowards break my resolve."

"What about our friends?" Mary asked.

"For the time being, you must tell no one that you're back or where you're staying."

"Even Hetty?" Mary asked.

"Especially Hetty, I'm afraid. No one really knows who set out to ruin us, but I'm sure they were Loyalists disguised as Patriots. If you do happen to meet and she asks, you know nothing."

"That's true enough, at least," Mary said. "I pray that in this case, not knowing will be protection enough."

As the cabriolet neared Philadelphia and her new quarters, Mary yawned, closed her eyes, and pretended to sleep. She wanted to think about Adam and how she might be able to let him know where she was if he came back to Philadelphia.

No, she corrected herself, *when* he came back. At the moment, how Adam might find her was of greater concern than her material losses.

❧

Adam returned to Philadelphia with two letters of recommendation, one to a friend of Ian MacPherson's who ran a dray business in the city, and another to the widow McAnally, who sometimes rented her spare room to recommended Christian gentlemen. Arriving late in the afternoon, Adam decided to seek lodging first.

"I reckon ye'll do if the minister says so," the widow said, eyeing Adam's buckskins with doubt. "I don't put up wi' drinkin' an' carousin'," she warned.

"I am glad to hear it. Neither do I, ma'am." Adam's sincerity so convinced his new landlady that she hurried away to prepare his supper.

The next morning Adam called on the drayman, a wiry man of middle years who was so glad to see someone actually asking to work that Adam was sure he would have been hired without the minister's letter.

"So many o' the young men are goin' for th' army now," he said. "Can y' start right away?"

"Later today, perhaps, but I'm concerned about finding some friends whose home burned whilst I was away. Might you know John Andrews, by any chance?"

A guarded look came over the man's face. "Everyone knows that he was burned out not long back."

"Yes. I heard he hadn't been hurt. Might you know where I could find him?"

"No, but in his place, I'd ha'e left town altogether. I'll count on havin' ye back here after noon."

"I'll be here." Adam shook Mr. Scott's hand, then turned back to the main street. Throngs of people were about, all total strangers. Adam might wish to meet Mary Andrews on the street, but he knew that was unlikely. However, there was one person in Philadelphia who should be able to help him find Mary, and soon he found someone to direct him to General Hawkins' house.

The reaction of the maid who answered the door reminded Adam of his first visit to Mary's home. After giving his name, Adam was invited into the Hawkins house. In the elegant drawing room, Hetty's mother greeted him with interest.

"So you are the frontiersman that Hetty wanted to invite to my husband's gala," she said. "Hetty will be so sorry to miss you—she went shopping this morning."

"That's all right, ma'am. I just got back to Philadelphia and saw that the Andrews' house had burned. I thought perhaps you might know where the family lives now."

Helen Hawkins frowned slightly. "A terrible business, that was. I understand that Patriots destroyed their warehouse, too. But I cannot tell you where the Andrews are now."

Adam felt keenly disappointed. "I thought perhaps you'd know, since your daughter and Mistress Mary are such good friends."

Mrs. Hawkins looked faintly annoyed as she stood, signaling that she wished Adam to leave. "I'm sorry I can't help you, Mr.—?"

"Craighead," Adam said, although he was fairly certain she couldn't have forgotten his name so quickly. "Would you please tell Hetty that I asked? I've taken lodgings near the market. I'll be working for Samuel Scott."

Mrs. Hawkins wrinkled her nose as if she smelled something unpleasant. "The drayman?"

"Yes, ma'am. Mistress Hawkins can ask for me there."

"Good day, Mr. Craighead."

"You will tell her, won't you?" he persisted, but Mrs. Hawkins turned to the maid who had just reappeared.

"Mr. Craighead is leaving. Please see him out."

Once outside, Adam realized he had gleaned no new information except for Mrs. Hawkins' strange statement that the

Patriots had caused the fires.

She knows more than she's willing to tell me, he thought, and wondered why. Perhaps she feared that he intended to pay suit to her daughter. Such an idea might once have struck Adam as funny, but under the circumstances, it merely added to his anger and frustration.

Adam retreated down the street to a point where he would be out of sight but could still see anyone who approached the Hawkins house. Mrs. Hawkins had told him that Hetty was shopping. If so, she should soon be home—the sun was almost directly overhead, signaling that the noon hour was at hand. He folded his arms across his chest and prepared to wait.

"Is that you, Mr. Craighead?"

A voice behind Adam startled him, and he turned to see Hetty Hawkins walking toward him, a small parcel tucked under one arm.

"Yes, ma'am—I went to your house, but your mother said you were out."

Hetty turned her blue eyes to his and smiled. "How sweet of you to wait for me," she said. "Where's your friend? Can you come in and take luncheon with us?"

"David's still in Carolina, and I must get back to work. I saw that the Andrews' house had burned—a workman told me they were all right, but I'd like to pay my respects. Can you tell me where they're staying?"

Hetty's smile faded for an instant, then reappeared. "They? Perhaps you've come back to see John Andrews, then? His warehouse burned too, you know. I doubt that he'll be able to hire you now."

The daughter is more maddening than her mother, Adam thought. He forced himself to be civil. "Do you know where they are?" he repeated.

Hetty lowered her eyes and was silent for a moment. Then she lifted her chin and her eyes challenged his. "I cannot give you their address," she said.

"But you do know where they are?"

"If you want to see Mary—"

"Yes, I want to see her. Just tell me where she is—I won't tell anyone else."

Hetty put her hand on Adam's sleeve and applied slight pressure. "I can't tell you where she is, but I can ask her to meet you somewhere this evening."

"That is very kind of you," Adam managed to say. "How about the east side of the market?"

"What time?"

"Seven?"

Hetty shook her head. "That's too early—make it eight."

Adam inclined his head. "Eight it is. Thank you, Miss Hawkins."

Hetty moved her hand from his sleeve. Her lips curved in the familiar half-smile that reminded him of a cat who had just enjoyed a saucer of cream.

"You will tell her?"

Hetty laughed, a soft, musical sound low in her throat. "Of course. Welcome back to Philadelphia, Mr. Craighead."

seventeen

"I thought ye'd be back sooner," was all Samuel Scott said when Adam returned to the drayman's livery stable.

"I'll work hard enough to make up for it," Adam said.

"Did ye find what ye sought?" Scott asked, somewhat mollified by Adam's offer.

"No, but I expect to soon."

"Good. Now come and gi'e me a hand wi' this, lad. Th' load must be at the docks this afternoon."

As the day warmed, the work grew harder, but Adam didn't mind. At least it occupied the time before the scheduled meeting with Mary Andrews.

Suppose she doesn't come? Adam tried to suppress his fear that Mary might not want to see him. In the midst of such thoughts, Adam smiled, imagining Ian MacPherson shaking his head disapprovingly at the way Adam was fretting.

"Ye do all ye can on your own, lad, then ye ask the Lord to take the matter as far as is needed, an' make an end to it there. Worryin' is a sign that ye lack faith."

That's easy enough for Ian MacPherson to say, Adam thought that evening as he washed off the day's grime and exchanged his buckskins for osanburg knee-breeches. He put on the shirt Mary had mended, topped by a waistcoat, and worked his feet into the city-stiff buckled shoes that Ian MacPherson had insisted on giving him. With his hair smoothed back and tied with a black ribbon, Adam looked very much like any other young colonial ready to court his sweetheart.

"Goin' out, are ye?" his landlady asked when he came to supper.

131

"I thought I might. Is there aught you need from the market, ma'am?"

"Not at this hour, sir," she said gruffly. "Ye'd best watch yer step around there. At night the market's likely t' have cutpurses an' thieves—an' other kinds o' folks ye ought to be careful of."

"I'll be careful," Adam promised. "Thank you for your concern," he added with a smile.

Mrs. McAnally adjusted her mob cap and looked flustered. "Neverth'less, I expect ye in at a decent hour."

"I'll probably not be gone long," Adam said, hoping otherwise.

It was less than a mile from Adam's lodgings to the market, and he arrived before full dark, far earlier than the time Hetty had told him to be there. Adam paced back and forth near the edge of the market where he could see—and be seen by— anyone who came near. As twilight deepened into night, most of the market stalls closed and the earlier crowds faded away.

She's not coming, Adam thought when the night watchman came by for the second time and eyed him as if he might be up to no good. Adam had almost decided to leave when a hooded figure detached itself from the deepest shadows and glided toward him. His heart pounding in anticipation, Adam moved to meet her.

Neither spoke as they met in a mutual embrace. Adam was startled when he felt soft hands on his cheeks, pulling his face toward hers. As the girl tilted back her head in an invitation for him to kiss her, the cloak's hood fell away, revealing blond hair, pale in the moonlight. Adam dropped his arms and stepped back as if he had been slapped.

"You're not Mary Andrews!"

The girl's musical laugh left Adam no doubt as to her identity. "How soon would you have known if I hadn't lost my hood?" Hetty asked.

As soon as our lips touched, Adam thought. "Soon—you and Mistress Andrews are quite unalike. Where is she?"

Hetty replaced her hood and took Adam's hand. "Come along. We can sit over there."

Adam allowed her to lead him to a crude bench near a food-seller's stall, where the faint aroma of meat pies and cheeses still lingered. As soon as they reached the bench, Adam took his hand from Hetty's. Once more her distinctive laugh rang through the night air.

"Where is Mistress Andrews?" he repeated.

"Mary wouldn't come, but I'm here," Hetty said.

"Why wouldn't she come? What did she say?" Adam persisted.

"Oh, Mr. Craighead, don't sound so angry," Hetty said sweetly. "Mary had no idea that you were interested in her, you know."

"That was not my understanding, Miss Hawkins."

She leaned closer to Adam and spoke softly. "My name is Hetty. I would like you to call me that. And what should I call you?"

"Anything you like," Adam replied shortly. His surprise at seeing Hetty had been replaced by a growing hurt that Mary could dismiss him so lightly. *I didn't think she was like that,* he thought. Could he have been so mistaken about her feelings for him?

"Oh, Adam, I know you're disappointed." Hetty placed her hand on his forearm. "But it's for the best that you not see her again, since—" She broke off and glanced away as if she couldn't bear to go on.

"Since what?"

When Hetty didn't immediately reply, Adam put both his hands on her upper arms and applied slight pressure.

"I didn't want to tell you," Hetty said then, speaking in a rush, "but Mary is engaged to be married to a British soldier.

Under the circumstances—"

Adam felt as if he had been kicked in the stomach. He dropped his hands from Hetty's arms and leaned away from her.

"Are you sure?" he managed to ask.

Hetty nodded. "Yes, I'm afraid it's true. From the time they met, the captain and Mary have been inseparable."

"When are they to be married?" asked Adam.

"The date hasn't been set yet—you know, with the fires, it's been difficult to make plans. But they don't want to wait."

"I see," said Adam, who neither saw nor wanted to see. "You could have told me this morning. Why didn't you?"

Hetty reached for Adam's hands and folded hers around them. "Because I thought it was her place to tell you. For your sake, I'm sorry that she chose not to, but I did want to see you again."

"Why?" Adam asked, and again Hetty's soft laughter floated across the market.

"Because from the first moment I saw you, I wanted to know you better. Perhaps now we can—"

"No!" Adam pulled his hands away from hers and stood. "Tell Mary I must see her. I can have nothing else to say to you until I have seen her."

Hetty stood and faced him, her chin tilted. "All right, I'll give her your message. But don't hope for too much."

"Tell Mary I'll be here tomorrow night—same time and place."

Hetty nodded and sounded almost business-like. "Very well. You can depend on me, Mr. Craighead."

Can I? Adam wondered as Hetty Hawkins walked away. He supposed he should have offered to see her safely home, but she hadn't seemed to expect it. For that Adam was glad, absorbed as he was with his disappointment and hurt.

Surely Mary will come tomorrow night, Adam told himself,

without a great deal of hope that she would.

☙

"Are you sure you can spare this many of your things?" Mary asked. She hadn't been back in Philadelphia more than two days before she and Hetty had met at the dressmaker's, and after a tearful reunion, Hetty had insisted that Mary come home with her and choose some clothing from her own clothespress.

"Of course—I just had a final fitting on three new dresses. I don't really need these."

"They should see me through until Madame DuBois can finish my order," Mary said. "That is, as long as I don't go anywhere more formal than the market."

Hetty made a face and busied herself replacing the other dresses in the press. "There's certainly no danger of that. Anyone would have to be out of their mind to try to entertain formally in Philadelphia in the summer."

"I'm a bit surprised to see you and your mother still here," Mary said. "I thought you'd go to the shore as usual."

Hetty shook her head so vigorously that her curls bounced. "Not with the way things are now. Papa says there are too many Patriots around there now—and after what they did to you, I'm sure you understand why we must stay here."

The Patriots didn't do anything to us, Mary inwardly protested. *It was Loyalists pretending to be Patriots.* But it would be foolish to discuss such matters with Hetty.

"You haven't mentioned your suitors," Mary said to change the subject. "Polly tells me that you had an officer on either arm the last time she saw you."

Hetty's smile showed her dimple. "Yes, and several more awaiting their turns. But most have gone off for some kind of training with the Prussians. Philadelphia is practically deserted these days."

"I've seen those German troops around the city," Mary said. "I hear there are thousands of them."

"Perhaps. Not one can speak decent English, their teeth are very bad, and they keep to themselves."

Mary smiled at Hetty's recital, well able to imagine what might have occurred to cause her to be so emphatic. "I take it that you don't consider them to be suitor material, then?"

Hetty rolled her eyes heavenward. "Certainly not! But turnabout is fair play. You must tell me if you've heard from the handsome frontiersman—what was his name? Adam something?"

"Adam Craighead," Mary said, feeling foolishly reluctant to speak of him in Hetty's presence. "No, and since the fire he'd not know how to find me if he did come back to Philadelphia."

"That's a pity," Hetty murmured. "But cheer up, Merry. When Papa's regiment comes back to town, things will be more lively."

⁂

Adam waited until it was nearly dark to make his way to the market. He had dressed with the same care he had taken the evening before, but this time he felt far less confident.

He hadn't been there long when someone wearing a cloak like Hetty's appeared and walked toward him. Adam had a brief hope that Mary might have a similar cloak, but as the figure came closer, his heart sank.

"I tried, Adam, but I was too late," Hetty said before he could speak.

"What do you mean?"

Hetty looked at the ground as if what she had to say was too painful for her to watch him receive it. "She's gone, eloped with the captain. They went to New Jersey to be married."

"How do you know?" Adam asked.

Hetty raised her face and looked at him earnestly. "Polly told me," she said. "I'm sorry, Adam," she added, and took a step toward him. Her expression was filled with such pity and concern that Adam was convinced she was telling the truth.

"I'd like to talk to Polly," he managed to say. "Surely it can do no harm to tell me where I can find her."

"I'm afraid that won't be possible," Hetty said smoothly. "Polly was about to leave to join Mary. They will live near the captain's post for the time being, and since Mr. Andrews is no longer in the city, Polly thought her place was with Mary."

"Mr. Andrews has left Philadelphia? Where did he go?"

"Polly said he left just before Mary did, but she didn't know where he was going. There is talk that the Patriots are still seeking to do him harm."

"Do you have an address for Mary in New Jersey?" Adam asked.

Hetty sounded faintly exasperated. "You frontiersmen are a stubborn lot, aren't you? Even if I knew the address—which I don't—it would be quite useless for you to attempt to contact Mary. She and the captain are obviously very much in love, and—"

"Never mind," Adam muttered. He'd already heard more than he wanted about that subject.

Hetty took a step forward and laid a sympathetic hand on Adam's arm. "I'm sorry, Adam. But perhaps you will allow me to be your friend."

Adam looked at Hetty's pleading eyes, aware only that she wasn't Mary. It was too soon to think past that. "Thank you," he said huskily.

eighteen

"Miss Merry, I'm leavin' for the market now. Is there anything special you'd like me t' get for y'?" Polly spoke from the door of the small room that Mary occupied in the rented house where they'd been living since their return from Lancaster.

Mary looked up from her needlework and shrugged. "Not really. Is it wise to go to the market in such threatening weather?"

"Th' rain may hold off a time. Anyhow, we must ha'e food."

"Then hurry," Mary said. "See if you can find a decent fowl for our supper."

"I'll try. Goodbye, mistress."

With her shopping basket over her arm, Polly hurried to the market, a sprawling rectangle where all manner of goods and foodstuffs were bought and sold year round. She made her selections as quickly as she could and had started back when a peal of thunder announced a downpour. Polly stepped back from the street and sought shelter in the overhang of a nearby shop. Through the ropes of falling rain, she watched in amusement as a drayman urged on his horse, which had halted in the middle of the road and refused to budge.

"Give 'im a taste o' th' whip, lad!" a bystander called, and when the drayman turned to see who had spoken, Polly found herself staring into the face of Adam Craighead—or a man who could be his twin.

At the same moment, Adam saw and recognized her. Immediately he joined her.

"Y' shouldn't leave th' wagon, sir," Polly cautioned.

"That horse isn't going anywhere—every time it rains, he stops until he's sure I'm drenched to the skin before he'll move again."

"I'm right surprised t' see y'," Polly said. "Mistress Mary was a-wonderin' where y' an' Master McKay were."

"Davy is still in Carolina. I heard about—I heard what happened," Adam said, finding it too painful to be more specific.

"'Twas a terrible time, but praise God no one was hurt," Polly said, and Adam realized she was referring to the fire.

"Yes, I know about that too—but I'm talking about Mistress Mary."

Polly looked puzzled. "Nothin' has happened t' her that I know of."

"She's gone to New Jersey, hasn't she?"

Polly's eyes opened wide in astonishment. "New Jersey?" she repeated. "Whyever would y' think Miss Merry went there?"

Adam felt the blood rushing to his face and he had to fight for self-control. "She isn't married, then?"

Polly shook her head vigorously. "No, sir. Where'd y' get that idea?"

"Someone told me," Adam said, feeling it was better to leave Hetty out of it. "I've been trying to find out where you were staying, but no one seemed to know."

"That's because the master fears th' men may come back," Polly said. "He tells Miss Merry that everything will be all right, but I know better."

"Where is she, Polly? I must see her."

Her eyes narrowed and she shook her head. "I'm not t' tell, sir. Master Andrews wouldn' like it."

"But surely you must know that I'd do nothing to harm her."

"I'll tell her y' said so," Polly said. "Th' rain's slacked and y' must get th' wagon out of th' way." Before Adam could move to stop her, Polly turned and fled. Regretfully he returned to his work, his mind churning.

Somehow Adam managed to get through the rest of the day. His relief in knowing that Mary wasn't married was no less intense than his disgust with himself that he had so readily believed it. As soon as he had finished his work, Adam went directly to Hetty's house, not taking time to change out of his work-stained buckskins.

"Tell Mistress Hawkins that Adam Craighead wants to see her," he said.

Hearing his voice, Mrs. Hawkins came to the door. "My daughter does not wish to see you, Mr. Craighead," she said firmly.

"That isn't what she told me, ma'am," Adam said, but the door closed in his face before he had finished speaking.

Now what do I do?

Adam walked back to his lodgings, his thoughts dark. That Hetty had deceived him was bad enough, but Polly Smith's refusal to divulge where Mary lived was even worse. There was one glimmer of hope. If Polly told Mary that she'd seen him, there weren't so many draymen in the city that she wouldn't be able to locate him.

If Mary is meant to be with me, please let her find me soon, Adam prayed as he drifted off to sleep.

⁂

It was raining hard when Mary opened the door to admit Hetty shortly after Polly had left for the market. "What brings you out on such a terrible day?" she asked.

Hetty took off her cloak and shook it before hanging it on the hall tree. "I have something to tell you," she said, and from her tone Mary knew it must be important.

"Come into the parlor. I'd offer you refreshment, but Polly's gone to the market."

Hetty sat beside Mary on the sofa. "I'm glad she's not here. What I have to tell you must be between us for the time being."

"Has something happened?" Mary asked, trying to imagine what could cause Hetty such concern.

"Yes, but I've been afraid to tell you."

"Tell me what?" Mary prompted.

"That Adam Craighead and I are in love."

Mary felt stunned, then incredulous. "That is a poor jest—" she began.

"No, it's true," Hetty said in a rush. "He came back just after you went to Lancaster, and naturally when he saw the house had burned, he came to me to find out what had happened. I told him that you were safe, then he—that is, we—"

Hetty broke off, too overcome to continue, and began sobbing into a lace handkerchief she kept on hand for such an emergency.

"Why did you wait until now to tell me?" Mary asked, her voice cold. "Why didn't you say something when I came back from Lancaster?"

Hetty continued sobbing into her handkerchief, muffling her reply. "Well, at f. . .first I didn't know where to find you, and then when we met, I. . .I just couldn't! I. . .I knew how h. . .h . . .hurt you'd be."

"Hurt!" Mary exclaimed. She stood and paced the floor, looking away from Hetty's teary face. "It's much deeper than that, Hetty. I thought you were my friend."

"Oh, Mary, I am!" Hetty rose and put out a hand in supplication. "But Adam and I, w. . .we couldn't help ourselves, and now Mama refuses to let him in the house—"

"I don't want to hear about it," Mary said. She took Hetty's cloak from the hall tree and thrust it toward her. "Just go and leave me alone."

"We may have to elope," Hetty said as she shrugged into the cloak. "Adam says he can't stand to be without me—"

Fighting the impulse to cover her ears, Mary took Hetty's arm and all but dragged her to the door. "Out!"

"I'd hoped you'd understand," Hetty cried as Mary closed the door in her face.

Trembling with rage and hurt, Mary went to her room and threw herself on the bed, racked by the most intense suffering she'd felt since her mother's death. Losing her home and knowing her father was still in peril had been hard to bear, but then Mary had still clung to the hope that Adam Craighead would come back and that they could face the future as one. Now, Mary had lost not only that hope, but her best friend, as well.

How could God let such a thing happen to me? Mary cried into the silence. Only her own sobs could be heard in reply.

❧

Adam still hoped that Mary would seek him out, but in case she didn't, he determined to find her through Polly Smith. He spent as much time around the market as he could that day, hoping that she might happen by. When she didn't, he inquired of several merchants until he found a stall-keeper who knew her.

"A scrawny little dark-haired thing, ain't she?" the poultry seller said in response to Adam's query. "Works for the man what got burnt out last month."

"Yes, that's the one—do you know where she lives?"

"No, but I'll tell her y' asked—she oughter be right glad t' know that."

Adam shook his head. "No, I want to surprise her. I'll make it worth your while to get her address," he added, seeing the uncertainty on the old woman's face.

"Well, why didn't y' say so in the first place? I'll ask

around—stop by this evenin' an' mayhap I'll have news for y'."

❧

By the time Mary heard Polly return, she'd cried until she had no more tears left. Not wanting Polly to see her red-rimmed eyes and pale cheeks, Mary told her she was resting.

"I have a headache and I'd like to be left alone," she said through the closed door.

"Y'd best hear what I have t' say," Polly replied. "I ha'e important news."

Mary walked to her bedroom door, but she didn't open it. "I'm in no mood to be riddled," she warned.

"I'm not riddlin' y'. Let me in, Miss Merry. This is important."

The urgency in the girl's voice made Mary fear that something had befallen her father. "It had better be," she muttered as she opened the door. Although Mary immediately turned away, Polly's gasp told her she had seen the grief written in her face.

"What's wrong, Miss Merry?" Polly entered the room and followed Mary to the lone window, where she stood with her back to Polly.

"I told you I have a headache. Just give me your news and leave me to die in peace."

Polly's lips twitched, and she nodded approvingly. "Well, Miss Merry, if y' can make a jest, I s'pose things can't be all that bad."

Mary turned to face Polly, her expression grim. "I'm not jesting. If you really have nothing to tell me—"

"But I do, Miss Merry—an' it's welcome news."

Mary sighed and folded her arms. "I'm listening."

Polly leaned forward, her eyes shining. "Well, if y' noticed, it did rain buckets soon 's I'd left fer th' market. I was shelterin' in front o' a shop when I looked up an' saw a drayman tryin' to get his horse t' move."

"Get to the point, Polly," Mary prompted when the girl paused.

"I'm tryin', Miss Merry—this drayman an' I looked at one another, an' straight off I saw who 'twas." Polly paused for dramatic effect, then grinned. "Adam Craighead—th' frontiersman himself."

"That is your welcome news?" Mary said bitterly. Through eyes that were beginning to fill with more tears, Mary saw the puzzled look on Polly's face.

"He's been tryin' t' find y' ever since he got back from Carolina. I thought y'd be pleased t' know it."

Mary took a deep breath and brushed away the tears with the back of her hand. "I hope you didn't tell him where we live."

Polly shook her head. "No, mistress. I wanted t', he seemed so anxious t' see y', but I recalled what the master said about not tellin' anyone, so I didn't. But I think I know how y' can find him."

Mary walked past Polly and sat down on the bed. "I doubt that Mr. Craighead wants to see me, and I certainly have no wish to see him. Now please go away and leave me alone."

"But, Miss Merry—"

"Go!" Mary ordered.

"I'll bring y' a poultice for y'r head," Polly said.

The damp cloth, saturated with fragrant herbs, eased Mary's throbbing temples, but otherwise brought her no comfort. She tried to put Adam and Hetty from her mind, but succeeded only in summoning vivid mental images of them together.

Hetty's perfect skin and blue eyes had captured many men's hearts, but Mary had thought Adam would be immune to her friend's charms. Apparently she had been badly mistaken. Hetty's way of dealing with men was so foreign to Mary that it had never occurred to her to imitate the other girl.

Maybe I should have, she thought forlornly. But Adam had seemed to be genuinely fond of her. *A man who can change his allegiance so quickly isn't worth a single tear.*

Yet Polly said that Adam wanted to see her. Why? To tell her he had fallen in love with her best friend? *No, thank you, Mr. Craighead.* She was far better off without him, Mary told herself, but her heart had not yet agreed.

❧

Slowed by the downpour, Adam was late getting his work done that day. When he had finally delivered his last load, he hurried to the market without taking time to change his clothes. One look at the poultry seller's face told Adam that her mission had been successful.

"I know where y' can find th' servant girl y' seek," she said. She bit the offered coin and satisfied herself that it was genuine before she spoke again. "Y'll need t' act fast—word is the fam'ly's about t' leave town."

"Where are they going?" he asked, but the woman shook her head. "All I can tell y' is they're now stayin' on Thimble Lane, near the tannery. Y' can't miss it if y' follow yer nose."

Adam returned to his lodgings, where he ate supper in haste before changing into his best clothes.

"Y' must be plannin' somethin' special tonight, Mr. Craighead," Mrs. McAnally said when Adam emerged from his room.

"Yes, ma'am. I'm going to see a very special young lady."

The woman smiled. "Well, ye look very keen. Th' lady ought t' be proud t' take yer arm."

"I hope so," Adam said.

Mary had never seen him geared out in osanburg. What she would think of it was the least of Adam's concerns as he made his way toward Thimble Lane.

nineteen

Adam pinched his nostrils shut as he passed the tannery and turned into Thimble Lane. It was a narrower street than the one on which the Andrews had formerly lived, and obviously occupied by far less prosperous residents. *Perhaps the fires had reduced John Andrews to poverty,* Adam thought, *as well as forcing him to hide from those who might still seek to do him harm.*

Adam stopped and looked around, but no one was about on the streets, and the poultry seller hadn't told him in which house the Andrews lived. He stood uncertainly in the middle of the street for a moment, then a man emerged from a house halfway down the block and came toward him. When he came close enough to hear him, Adam spoke.

"Good evening. I'm looking for a family that just moved to Thimble Lane, a man and his daughter. Might you know where I could find them?"

The man regarded Adam with obvious suspicion. "Why d' y' want t' know?"

"They're my friends. I just came back from Carolina and heard that they're in these parts."

"Carolina, is it?" The man's eyes narrowed. "How feels that colony about war wi' Britain?"

Aware that the question was some sort of test, Adam shrugged. "About as in Pennsylvania. People expect there could be a fight."

"And who will win it?"

"Only God knows that," Adam replied with sincere conviction.

"Mebbe," the man replied. "Try the last house on the left—they may be th' ones y' seek."

"Thank you kindly, sir." Adam touched his forehead in a brief salute, then hurried to the end of the block.

The house on Thimble Lane lacked a knocker, but Adam rapped on it with a force that brought an immediate response.

"Who's there?" a cautious voice on the other side called out.

"Adam Craighead. Is that you, Miss Polly?"

The door opened, and once more Polly Smith seemed surprised to see Adam.

"How did y' find us?" she asked.

"Never mind that. I'm here to see Mistress Mary."

Polly frowned and looked up and down the street. "I hope nobody a-followed y'."

"I'm sure they didn't. Please tell your mistress I'm here."

Polly shook her head. "I don't think she'll see y', but wait there an' I'll ask."

The servant girl left Adam standing on the doorstep as the summer twilight darkened to night. When she returned, Mary's answer was written in her face. "It's as I said—she won't see y'."

"Why not? Did she say?"

"T' tell th' truth, Miss Mary's not herself just now. She was fine when I went t' th' market, but by th' time I got back t' tell her I'd seen y', she'd been cryin' an' wouldn' tell me why."

"What did she say when you told her you'd seen me?"

"That she wanted nothin' t' do wi' y'. Then she said she had a headache an' wanted t' be left alone. Until just now, I hadn't spoken t' her since."

"I think I know what might be wrong," Adam said. "If you'll just let me see her, I'm sure we can straighten out this. . .misunderstanding."

Polly shook her head. "It wouldn' be any use for y' t' see

Miss Merry t'night. Let her get some rest and y' come back t'morrow—by then mayhap she'll be seein' things some different."

Every impulse urged Adam to brush past Polly and find Mary, take her into his arms, and tell her he loved her. But no matter how much he longed to see Mary, Adam realized that forcing his way might only make matters worse. He had a pretty good idea that Hetty Hawkins was somehow behind Mary's sudden change of heart, and he intended to get her to admit it.

"Perhaps you're right," Adam said. "I'll be back tomorrow, and I *will* see her then."

Polly nodded and looked relieved. "I'm glad t' hear it. Good evening, Master Craighead."

Adam strode away, wishing he had thought to ride his horse. It was some distance to the Hawkins' house, and the only way he knew to get there was to return to the market and start from there. By the time Adam had done so, it was already past the hour when many households retired for the evening.

At the Hawkins' house, lights gleamed from almost every window. As Adam approached the front door and glanced in at the front window, he saw figures moving about in the drawing room. *Something unusual is happening,* he thought. Perhaps the general's duties had brought him back to Philadelphia, and the household had stayed up late to welcome him. Adam preferred not to see General Hawkins, who hadn't seemed to care for him very much, but he would if he had to do so to reach Hetty.

Resolutely Adam knocked. To his surprise, General Hawkins himself opened the door. His brow furrowed as if he found Adam's face familiar, but had no name to match it.

"Adam Craighead, sir. We met at the Andrews' house several months past."

"Who is it?" Adam heard Mrs. Hawkins call.

General Hawkins turned from Adam to answer her. "It's no

one to be concerned about, dear. I'll be back in a moment." Then he addressed Adam. "If you've come to enlist, I can direct you to the proper place."

"No, sir. This is a personal matter."

General Hawkins looked faintly annoyed. "Oh? What personal business have you with this household?"

"I must see your daughter, sir. I know it's late—" Adam began, but the general interrupted him.

"Hetty has retired for the evening. If you wished to see her, you should have called at a decent hour."

While her father was still speaking, Hetty appeared and took his arm. "I'm still up, Papa. Do let Mr. Craighead come inside, since he's already here."

General Hawkins shrugged. "Very well, but only for a short while. We must all rise early."

"Come in here." Hetty pulled Adam into a small parlor off the drawing room and closed the door behind her. Immediately she reached out to put her arms around his neck, but Adam caught her wrists and held them as he glared at her. "What—" she began.

"I want to know what you told Mary about me," Adam said.

"Let go—you're hurting me," Hetty protested.

"Not until you answer me," Adam said grimly. "I want the truth."

"I'll scream and Papa will have you arrested," Hetty threatened.

"I'm sure you would, at that." Adam released Hetty's wrists and folded his arms across his chest. "You seem to be rather good at lying."

Hetty's face reddened. "Oh, Adam, don't be angry. Everything I did was for you—"

"Stop it!" he exclaimed. He clenched his fists in an attempt to stifle the urge to shake Hetty until her teeth rattled. "I want to know what you told Mary."

Hetty's lower lip trembled, and tears spilled from her blue eyes. "I told her I'd seen you," she said.

"That isn't all, is it? What else did you say?"

Hetty looked down at the floor and wrung her hands. "I meant no harm, Adam. I just thought if she knew how we felt about each other—"

"What!" Adam stepped forward and put his hands atop her shoulders. "You told her I cared for you?"

Hetty looked miserable. "I know you would have, Adam, if you had the chance. Just because Mary saw you first—"

Adam dropped his arms to his sides and shook his head. "I don't want to hear anything more about that. You must go with me to Mary's house and tell her the truth—if any truth's in you at all."

Again the color rose in Hetty's cheeks. "I meant every word that I said to Mary. If you won't return my affection, then it's your loss."

"You won't apologize to Mary, then?"

Hetty shook her head. "No. What happened was a misunderstanding, that's all. I'm thankful I saw your true nature in time—if Mary's fool enough to want you, she's welcome to you."

"Hetty! Are you in there with Mister Craighead? Come out this minute!"

At the sound of her mother's voice, Hetty turned and opened the door. "Yes, Mama. Mr. Craighead's just leaving. He won't be coming back."

Mrs. Hawkins looked at Adam almost triumphantly. "I told you that he wasn't suitable for you," she said. "Now you see that I was right."

Hetty's smile was barely more than a smirk. "Yes, Mama. Goodbye, Mr. Craighead."

Adam decided to try one last appeal. "If you should change your mind about seeing Mistress Ma—" he began, but Hetty interrupted him.

"I won't. Mama and I are leaving Philadelphia tomorrow to go to Papa's headquarters in New York." Hetty seemed to relish Adam's surprise.

"Then I wish you a safe journey, ma'am," Adam said, half bowing to Mrs. Hawkins.

Somehow Adam managed to get out of the Hawkins' house without saying anything he might later regret, although his mind was still seething with dark thoughts about Hetty when he approached his lodgings and saw that a cabriolet had stopped in front of the house.

That looks like the Andrews' carriage—Maybe Mary changed her mind and has come to see me. Adam quickened his steps and arrived at the carriage just as its occupant stepped down from it.

"Good evening, Adam," John Andrews said.

Adam tried to hide his disappointment. "Mr. Andrews—I thought you were out of town."

"So I was, and soon will be again. Get into the carriage, lad. We must talk."

Surprised, Adam did as he was told, and the cabriolet headed back toward the market. "How did you know where to find me?"

"The drayman Scott directed me here. Had I known you were in the city, you could have been working for me instead."

"When I came back and found you'd been burned out, I went to Neshaminy. The Reverend MacPherson saw to it that I had work and a place to stay while I looked for you. It was only today that I discovered your lodgings."

"I don't aim to be easily found," John Andrews said. "But I'm glad to see you, lad. I need your help."

"In what way?"

"For the next few days, at least, someone must look after Mary."

Adam was glad the darkness masked his expression. "Is something wrong?"

"Aye, the same thing that was wrong before I was burned out. Those Loyalist rascals won't rest until they stop me from trading goods for the Patriots' use. It's too dangerous for my daughter to stay in Philadelphia, but they also know where to find us in Lancaster."

"What will you do then, sir?"

"That remains to be seen. In the meantime, I want Mary to leave the city tonight."

"So soon?" Adam asked.

"Yes. The Loyalists know where we are now, and this time I fear they might do harm to my daughter. I know she likes you, Adam. I want her to be in a safe place until I can arrange to move my operations elsewhere."

Adam was having difficulty comprehending what John Andrews had apparently already planned. "You're asking me to take Mary somewhere?"

"Yes. I can't spare Thomas just now, and I'm sure you can use a rifle if you have to. Furthermore, I can trust my daughter with you. Will you help us?"

"I already have a job. The drayman—" Adam began, but John Andrews interrupted him.

"I've already spoken to Scott and to your landlady, as well. We all agree that you should take Mary to Neshaminy. Ian MacPherson has been my friend for many years—he'll be glad to take her in."

Adam swallowed hard. "I'll help you any way I can, sir, but Mar—your daughter might not want to go with me."

"I doubt that. You know, Adam, God sent you here just when we needed you. I prayed that you'd decide to come back."

It was a moment before Adam could speak. "I prayed to be shown the right path. I'm still not sure about everything, but for now I'll do whatever I can to help you."

"Good. Here we are. Wait in the parlor. I'll tell Polly to waken Mary."

Mary had fallen asleep before supper, and Polly didn't have the heart to wake her up. Several times Mary had roused briefly, only to remember afresh the pain that Hetty's visit had brought. She closed her eyes tightly and willed herself back into a troubled sleep. Once she imagined that she heard Adam's voice, and another time she thought that her father had come home. She could hear him conversing in low tones with Polly, but she was too weary to get up. Moments later, all was quiet and Mary had slept once more.

Now, however, the voices were loud and insistent, and Mary sat upright and listened in the darkness for some hint of what was happening. There was a light rap on her door, and Polly entered, bearing a single candle.

"What's all the racket about?" Mary asked. Her mouth felt dry and her chest ached from weeping.

"Master Andrews is back, Miss Merry. He wants us t' get ready to leave town."

Mary swung her feet over the side of the bed and frowned. "Tonight?"

"Yes, mistress. Y' might want t' change that gown, since y've been sleepin' in it. I'm t' pack your things."

Fully awake, Mary stuffed her feet into her kid slippers. "I can't believe Papa'd expect us to travel to Lancaster in the middle of the night!" she exclaimed. "Has something happened?"

"I don't know, mistress," Polly answered. "But you'd best take a bite o' supper before we go, and y' can see what he has t' say."

Mary looked down at her day dress and decided it would make no sense to change it, only to have whatever she put in its place even more wrinkled by the jostling carriage. "If I have to travel, it'll be in this," she said.

"Wait, Miss Merry. Let me get th' tangles from your hair, at least."

"No one will see it," Mary said, but she sat at her dressing-table and allowed Polly to ply the brush. A glimpse in the mirror showed Mary that her tears had done no lasting damage. The circles under her eyes might be deeper than usual, or merely shadows cast by the candle's light.

"Now you'll do," Polly said with satisfaction.

"Do for what?" Mary asked tartly, but Polly, gathering Mary's few remaining possessions, merely smiled.

Something is going on, Mary thought as she went down the stairs. Polly seemed entirely too pleased with herself.

"Papa?" she called when she reached the hallway. A light glowed in the sitting-room, and Mary walked toward it, fully expecting to see her father. Instead, a man outfitted in osanburg knee breeches stood in the middle of the room, someone as tall as Adam Craighead. Then he stepped forward and Mary let out a cry of surprise.

"Adam Craighead! What are you doing here? I told Polly I didn't want to see you."

"Your father brought me here tonight, but I'd have come back tomorrow and stayed until I made you listen to me."

Mary half-turned as if to leave. "What could you possibly have to say that you think I would want to hear?"

Adam forced himself to stay where he was, his eyes riveted on hers. "Only one thing. I love you, Mary. I always have, and God willing, I always will."

Mary brought her hands together and steepled her fingers. "'Tis a strange way you have of showing it, asking my best friend to marry you," Mary said.

Adam went to Mary and put his hands loosely on her upper arms. "I never asked Hetty to marry me. I went to her to try to find out where you were, and she told me you'd gone to New Jersey to marry a British officer. She lied to us both."

Mary had been standing still and tensed, keeping her distance. As he spoke, Mary looked deeply into Adam's eyes and knew that he spoke the truth. Tears came to her eyes, and Mary stepped forward and rested her head on his shoulder. "Hetty was always my best friend. How could she do such a wicked thing to us?"

Adam tightened his arms around Mary and moved his lips against her forehead, soothing her as a father might a fretful child. "Hush. Don't waste your tears on Mistress Hetty. The selfish always come to grief, and usually by their own scheming."

"I don't want to think about her ever again," Mary murmured.

"Then don't," Adam said. "Think of us instead."

"Don't talk—just shelter me here in your arms forever."

Adam smiled and looked down at Mary. With his thumb, he brushed away her most recent tears. "You haven't said you love me," he said.

Mary pulled away from his embrace and tilted her head to one side. "I wouldn't have cried over you if I didn't love you."

"I know," Adam replied. He bent his lips to hers in a tender kiss that ended only when John Andrews entered the room and cleared his throat loudly.

"We must go now."

Mary turned without embarrassment to face her father. "Papa, Adam has something to ask you."

Adam looked surprised, then he realized what Mary must mean. "Sir, I would like permission to seek your daughter's hand."

Conflicting emotions vied in John Andrews' face before he held out a hand to each of them. "It appears that your request is somewhat after the fact, but I shall take it under consideration."

"Oh, Papa! Go ahead and tell Adam you'll be glad to have

me settled—I've heard you say it often enough!"

Polly stuck her head into the room, and from her pink cheeks and bright eyes, it was clear that she'd probably been in the hallway for some time. "Master, Thomas says we'd best go now."

"Very well." Mr. Andrews released his daughter's and Adam's hands. "Thomas will drive you all to Mr. Craighead's lodgings, then take you and Polly on to Neshaminy and bring the carriage back. I'll go on to Lancaster then."

Mary turned puzzled eyes to her father. "What about Adam?"

"He can ride his own horse to Neshaminy at first light," John Andrews said. "Adam will keep me informed of your whereabouts until I've found a safe place for us to live."

"I suppose I'm in your employ, then?" Adam questioned.

"Of course. I can't very well let my daughter be courted by a drayman."

Mary hugged her father, then silently they went out into the starless night.

twenty

After the carriage had gone on to Neshaminy, John Andrews sat in the parlor of Adam's lodgings and told him that he was almost certain that someone had told a Loyalist spy where to find him. Immediately Adam thought of a likely suspect.

"Might Mary's friend Hetty Hawkins have given you away?"

John Andrews looked thoughtful. "I would like to think not, but it's possible that Hetty could have made some innocent remark about us that was passed on to General Hawkins."

"I don't trust the girl," Adam said. "She told both Mary and me rather serious falsehoods."

Mary's father sighed. "That doesn't surprise me. I always knew that Hetty was more worldly than Mary, but I never thought she was dishonest. If I had, I wouldn't have permitted their friendship."

"Hetty and her mother are leaving town tomorrow."

"Would that they had sooner," John Andrews muttered. "Get you on to bed now. We've much traveling ahead of us."

Adam rose before dawn, gathered his few possessions, and left without awakening John Andrews, who was sleeping on the parlor sofa. Mrs. McAnally seemed genuinely sorry to see him go, and after asking him to tell Ian MacPherson to send her another such lodger, she pressed Adam's hand and told him she'd pray for him. "I think the Lord has great things in store for y'," she said firmly. "I hope y' can let Him have His way."

"So do I," Adam told her, but as he rode toward Neshaminy, he wondered how much of what had happened was due to his feelings for Mary, and how much to being under God's direction. *Mary is the right wife for me, I'm sure of it,* Adam thought, but he still felt no special purpose for his life.

In the early morning quiet, Adam prayed intensely, *I still seek Your sign, Lord, and I will be obedient to it and to You.*

Soon afterward, Adam met Thomas returning with the Andrews' cabriolet. Thomas lifted his whip in greeting and called out that Mistress Mary and Miss Polly had safely reached the minister's. "Master Andrews waits for you at Mrs. McAnally's," Adam called back, then each rode on.

When he reached Neshaminy, Adam was greeted warmly by Ian MacPherson's wife.

"Mistress Andrews and the servant girl were very weary, so I sent them upstairs to rest," she said. "Come and eat now—the reverend will be back soon."

"Where is he?" Adam asked.

"Lecturing," she replied. "Hebrew or Greek or some such—I can't keep up with all that he teaches."

"Are there many ministerial students?"

Mrs. MacPherson glanced appraisingly at Adam. "As many as the Lord sends. I daresay there's always room for one more."

Mary and Polly were still upstairs when Ian MacPherson came home. He greeted Adam with affection, but also with a restraint that Adam had never before seen. "Come outside for a bit, Adam. I ha'e some news ye maun hear."

Something in his tone alarmed Adam, and even before he heard the minister's words, Adam felt a sense of foreboding.

Ian MacPherson took Adam to the crest of a small hill over-looking his house and the scattered buildings that made up the Neshaminy settlement. An ancient tree had been cut down the winter before, and the minister motioned for Adam to sit with him on its wide stump.

"You've had some word from my parents," Adam said, guessing the cause of the minister's concern.

"Yes, I'm afraid so. Your mother writes that your father has taken a turn for the worse."

Adam felt his heart tighten. "He always worked too hard."

"It seems that his time may be near. 'Twould mean much to him to see ye once more and to know that ye've settled at least part of your future."

Adam glanced sharply at Ian MacPherson, who smiled faintly. "Mistress Andrews told me that ye two have an understanding. I'm sure 'twill please your parents to know ye'll have such a worthy helpmeet."

"Her father and my mother were special friends," Adam said, not knowing how else to phrase it.

Ian MacPherson nodded. "I know the whole story," he said. "That their children should find one another is quite amazing."

"I think it's more than that," Adam said, and told the minister about his experience in North Carolina. "I don't know if it was really a sign, or whether I just wanted to believe it was," he concluded, "but it led me back to her."

"Aye, lad. I believe that ye ken it meant that, and even more. Now the question is, what will ye do about it?"

When Adam and the minister returned to the house, Mary and Polly were helping Mrs. MacPherson prepare supper. Seeing Adam, Mary ran to him and impulsively hugged him, then drew back as she realized that the minister and his wife might not approve of her behavior.

"I'm glad you got here safely," Mary said, and the compassion in her face told Adam that she knew about his father's illness.

"We need to talk," Adam said. "I know I promised to help your father, but I feel I must go to the Monongahela immediately."

Mary nodded and her eyes welled with sympathetic tears. "I understand. We'll have to pass through Lancaster on our way there, anyway—you can tell Papa what is happening then."

Adam looked at Mary in surprise. "We? Surely you're not thinking of going with me."

"Why not?"

"It—it wouldn't be proper," Adam blurted out.

"We're going to be married anyway—under the circumstances, Reverend MacPherson could suspend the banns and marry us here and now."

Adam shook his head. "No, Mary. We can't do that to your father. He deserves to see us wed."

"Well, married or not, I'm going with you, and that's that!" Mary announced.

Adam looked helplessly from Ian MacPherson to his wife and back to Polly, who was crying noisily into her apron. "Won't someone tell her she can't do this?"

Ian MacPherson took Adam's hand and squeezed it. "Oh, but she can, lad, and I believe she will. Ye can get a license in Lancaster, then John Andrews can go to the Monongahela with ye an' be present when Caleb Craighead hears your vows."

Adam and Mary looked at each other, and both nodded. "Yes," Adam said. "That would be the best. I just pray that we can get back to Father in time."

"Ye should be on your way as soon as ye can manage it," Ian MacPherson said.

Mary turned to the minister. "Will you pray for us first?"

"Of course. There's always time for that."

Ian MacPherson offered to loan them his carriage, but Adam wouldn't hear of it. "My horse is sturdy enough to carry Mary and me to Philadelphia, and Samuel Scott can find us a mount for Mary. We'll make much better time on horseback."

"I wish I could go wi' y', Miss Merry," Polly said mournfully.

"So do I, Polly, but we'll be back for you as soon as we can. In the meantime, you must make yourself useful to the reverend and his wife."

Mrs. MacPherson put her arm around Polly's slight shoulders. "Don't you worry a mite about that—we'll welcome her company."

A half hour later, with Mary riding pillion behind Adam, her arms holding him loosely around his waist, they returned to Philadelphia. There Adam left Mary with Mrs. McAnally while he found her a horse.

"I like y'r choice o' a wife," the woman whispered to Adam when he returned with a bay gelding for Mary.

"So do I," he replied.

As they left Philadelphia, Adam took comfort that Mary was at his side. Her presence couldn't take away the sadness of his father's illness, but her love and quiet understanding made it more tolerable.

"This is a fine horse Mr. Scott gave you," Mary told Adam. "I always wanted my own horse, but Papa kept putting me off about it."

"You ride quite well, though. Someone must have taught you."

Mary's lips pressed together in a grim line. "That someone was Hetty. We were closer than sisters for years. Now I can't bear to think of her."

"She could have done us both great harm, I'll admit, but she didn't succeed. We should forgive her and pray that she'll learn the error of her ways before it's too late."

Mary looked at Adam appraisingly. "Spoken like a true minister of the Gospel, but you don't know Hetty as well as I do. Many times over the years I tried to convince her that she needed spiritual guidance, but she never listened."

"What about her parents? Aren't they Christians?"

"I suppose they think they are, but their church-going always seemed to be a matter of who would see them and what they would wear, as if the services were just another social event."

"That's unfortunate."

"Yes, but there's nothing we can do about it. We're almost to Lancaster—it's time we considered how to persuade Papa to go on with us."

When the young couple found John Andrews and Adam explained the situation with Caleb Craighead, he welcomed their suggestion that they all travel to the Monongahela together.

"I haven't been this far west in many years," Mary's father said after they'd crossed the Susquehanna and Adam pointed out the way to Stone's Crossing. "I'd almost forgotten how much land there is out here."

"All of it hereabouts is occupied or claimed," Adam said. "Even as far west as the Monongahela, no big tracts are left."

"I ought to visit some of the merchants who've settled here. Perhaps we could work out some arrangement that would help us all."

"Oh, Papa! Does everything you do have to be connected with business?" Mary asked, and after that her father said no more, although Adam noticed that he seemed quite interested in every trading post they passed, particularly those on bodies of water.

Eventually the road became an ever-narrower trail, until at last they came into territory where Adam knew every path by heart. They rode single-file, with Adam in the lead, and the closer they came to Adam's village, the more silent and withdrawn he became.

"There should be someone about," he said when he stopped near the edge of a deep forest. "We haven't seen anyone for the last five miles—I don't like it."

"What could be the matter?" John Andrews asked.

"I don't know, but I'm going to ride ahead and see what's happening. You and Mary wait here."

The village was eerily quiet as Adam entered it. A few fires burning under cooking-pots testified that someone was still there, but no one tended them. Then as he approached the lodge of the chief, the low keening of the Death Song reached his ears, and Adam's blood ran cold. He dismounted and stood with his head bowed in sorrow, fearful that he had arrived too late.

"Adam! Is it really you?"

He turned as his mother came to his side, smaller and paler than he remembered, but her face remarkably calm and unlined. Wordlessly they embraced. "Thank God you're here," she said against his chest.

"What is this?" Adam asked. He released her and gestured toward the silent village.

Ann Craighead's eyes filled with tears. "'Tis the Lenni-Lenape's way of saying goodbye to their minister," she said thickly.

"I got word that Father was ill," Adam said. "I prayed we'd get here in time."

Ann looked questioningly at her son. "We? You're not alone?"

"No. John and Mary Andrews are with me."

Adam's mother put a hand to her throat and turned even paler. "John Andrews is here? Your father will be happy to see him."

Adam raised his head sharply. "He still lives?"

"Aye, but he's very weak. Perhaps ye should see him alone first."

"Take me to him, then."

Caleb Craighead rested in the cabin he had built many years before, and Adam's first impression was how small and wasted his father's large frame seemed. His father's hair had turned white, and his skin was almost as ashen. His eyes were closed, but when his wife spoke his name, Caleb opened them and looked directly into his son's face.

"Can it be ye, Adam?" he said with more vigor than Adam would have thought possible.

"Aye, Father. I've come to seek your blessing." Adam knelt beside his father and grasped his frail hands.

"That ye've always had, lad."

Adam's eyes filled with tears as his father raised a hand to Adam's forehead and murmured a prayer. Adam was unable to speak for a moment. "Someone came with me that you must meet," he finally managed to say. "Mother, can you fetch them? They're just at the edge of the forest."

"I'll send someone after them," Ann Craighead replied.

"I'm glad ye came back, son. I don't fear death, but I am concerned about ye."

"Don't be—God has taken care of me, and I have faith He always will. When I was in Carolina, I think He sent me a sign."

Caleb briefly inclined his head. "Go on," he whispered.

"I'd asked God to show me what I should do, and then I saw a pair of eagles. Joshua and Sarah told me there were no eagles in that part of Carolina, but I know what I saw."

"What d'ye take the sign to mean?"

"I'm not sure, but there were two eagles, and I'm certain I've found the one God wants me to marry."

Caleb almost smiled. "That's an important decision, lad. Are ye so sure?"

Adam heard footsteps behind him and looked back to see Mary and her father enter the cabin. "Here she is, Father— you can see for yourself."

Caleb nodded at Mary, then looked past her to her father. Caleb extended both hands to him. "John Andrews—after all these years—"

"'Tis quite some time since the day an earnest young minister turned my life toward the Lord, but I'll never forget it—or you."

Caleb looked at Mary, who was struggling not to cry. "Is this your young lady, Adam?"

Adam took Mary's hand and drew her closer to his father's side. "Aye, sir. Her name is Mary Ann Andrews. We hope you'll perform our marriage."

Ann Craighead uttered a sharp cry and put a hand to her mouth. "Oh, Adam! I don't know if he has the strength."

"Of course I do!" Caleb said so fiercely that they all laughed. "Mary Ann, is it? Come here, child, and let me look at you."

Mary knelt beside Caleb and took one of his hands between hers. "I am honored to meet you, sir," she said.

"Are ye both sure ye know what ye're doing?" he asked her. "Marriage is a sacred bond, not to be lightly entered upon."

Mary inclined her head. "Adam and I know that," she said. "Will you marry us?"

Ann's eyes met her son's and she nodded. "Can ye hold the book, husband?" she asked.

Caleb closed his eyes and shook his head. "No need. I know the words here." He touched his chest, then opened his eyes. "Take the bride's hand, Adam—I trust that she won't bite ye."

Adam smiled. "I've heard those words often enough," he said, remembering the many times Caleb Craighead had said such words to couples who stood before him to be married. He turned to Mary and took her hand in his. "We've no ring," he said.

"Use mine." Ann Craighead slipped off her wedding band and handed it to Adam. When he hesitated, she thrust it into his palm and closed his fingers around it. "Just for the ceremony, of course. Ye maun get your own later."

"I suppose we're ready, then," Adam said.

"Let us pray," Caleb said, and the brief ceremony began.

※

They stayed in the village by the Monongahela for a week, time enough for Mary to meet Adam's Lenni-Lenape friends who were still in the village.

"So many have left," Adam remarked. Many of the young men had decided to cast their lot with a related clan by the headwaters of the Ohio, including the warrior who had wed Karendouah.

"Why do they go?" Adam asked his old friend Tel-a-ka, knowing what the answer would be.

"Hunting no good now. White man takes deer, takes buffalo, builds his villages where our ancestors always found meat."

"What will you do?" Adam asked.

Tel-a-ka shrugged. "The people talk of the land beyond the Endless Mountains. They say it is a fair country."

From his tone Adam knew Tel-a-ka didn't agree, but Adam knew the time might soon come when the Clan of the Bow would no longer be able to sustain itself where they were. "May God guide you, my brother," Adam said, and Tel-a-ka nodded.

"My people will do as we are led," he said.

As the week wore on, John Andrews had time to renew his friendship with Caleb and Ann before Caleb slipped into a peaceful sleep from which he did not awaken.

Tel-a-ka, as chief of the Clan of the Bow, took charge of the burial preparations, but when the time came for the body to be laid to rest in a quiet glen, it was Adam who delivered the funeral sermon and said the final prayers.

"Ye should go now," Ann Craighead said a few days later. "It was God's blessing that ye came when ye did, but I'll not ask ye to stay longer."

"I don't want to leave you here alone. Won't you come back with us?" Adam asked, suspecting what his mother's answer would be.

"Nay, son, I'm not alone. These are my people. They'll look after me."

"But more and more of the Lenni-Lenape are going away every year, Mother. It was Father's wish that we should take care of you."

"And I'll let you, when the time comes that I need it. But not now. There's too much of my life with your father in this place."

Adam kissed his mother's cheek. "I understand. But later you might change your mind. Will you promise to let me know when you're ready to leave?"

Ann nodded. "I promise."

John Andrews had been standing apart from the others, but now he joined them. "Adam, I know you can see Mary safely back to Lancaster without me. I believe I'll stay on a while and make some trade contacts in the area. That is, if I won't be imposing on you," he added to Ann.

Her cheeks showed brief color. "Of course not. The lodge where ye've been staying is yours for as long as ye like."

"What about your business, Papa?" Mary asked.

"I've enough laid by for such a time as this. There's not much I can do as long as the Loyalists watch my every move, anyway."

Ann Craighead put a hand on her son's shoulder. "From what I hear, it seems that war against the British is bound to come. Will ye and the family in Carolina join it?"

"If we have to defend what is rightfully ours, we will, but we're not seeking it."

Ann looked worried. "I would that the British were not either. I'll pray for ye all daily, that God'll protect ye."

"We'll await you in Lancaster," Mary said as she and her father said goodbye the next morning.

"Take your time, sir," Adam added, knowing how badly his mother would need a friend in the days ahead.

"God bless ye both," Ann called after them.

"Your mother is a fine woman," Mary said when they had

ridden some time in silence. "I can see why our fathers both loved her."

"Did you know you remind me of her?"

Mary looked surprised. "I don't look anything like your mother."

"Not in appearance, perhaps, but you're alike in spirit."

Mary reached out and touched Adam's hand. "That's the nicest compliment you could ever give me," she said.

The next day brought Adam and Mary to the tallest peak on the journey, and they stopped at its summit to rest their horses. The young couple sat with their backs to a rock, idly looking up at the cloudless blue sky. Suddenly, two huge birds flew over their heads.

"Eagles!" Mary whispered. She stood with Adam, and they held hands as they watched a magnificent pair of bald eagles soar overhead, alternately gliding and moving their powerful wings. "Where do you suppose they came from?" Mary craned her neck in a vain attempt to find their nest.

"Eagles always build in the tallest tree on the highest land," Adam said.

"Look! Now they're circling. They must see some prey."

Three times the magnificent birds formed arcs overhead, then in unison they slowly flew away in a slanting path that led south and east, and finally out of Mary's and Adam's sight.

Neither spoke for a long moment, then Adam drew Mary to him and held her for a moment against his heart. "Now I know what God wants me to do."

"The eagles were your sign?" she asked.

"I believe so. Did you note the path they took?"

"I'm not very good at directions. Weren't they going south?"

"Southeast—toward Carolina."

Mary looked puzzled. "Carolina? What's there?"

"People who need me. When I was there I didn't want to see it, but now it seems so clear—I'll have to prepare myself first, but—"

"You'll be a minister," Mary finished for him.

"Yes. Father was right—he always said I should be a minister, but I doubted I had a calling."

"I thought from the first that you had the gift for it—but I prayed that you'd decide to work for my father so you'd stay near me."

Adam searched Mary's face. "And now?"

"I want whatever God wants for you."

"For us both, Mary," he corrected, drawing her close to his heart again. "Like the eagles, we'll always be together."

A Letter To Our Readers

Dear Reader:

In order that we might better contribute to your reading enjoyment, we would appreciate your taking a few minutes to respond to the following questions. When completed, please return to the following:

Rebecca Germany, Editor
Heartsong Presents
P.O. Box 719
Uhrichsville, Ohio 44683

1. Did you enjoy reading *Sign of the Eagle*?
   ☐ Very much. I would like to see more books
     by this author!
   ☐ Moderately
     I would have enjoyed it more if _____

   _____

2. Are you a member of *Heartsong Presents*? Yes   No
   If no, where did you purchase this book? _____

   _____

3. What influenced your decision to purchase this
   book? (Check those that apply.)

   ☐ Cover   ☐ Back cover copy

   ☐ Title   ☐ Friends

   ☐ Publicity   ☐ Other _____

4. On a scale from 1 (poor) to 10 (superior), please rate the following elements.

___Heroine   ___Plot

___Hero   ___Inspirational theme

___Setting   ___Secondary characters

5. What settings would you like to see covered in *Heartsong Presents* books?

_____

_____

6. What are some inspirational themes you would like to see treated in future books?_____

_____

_____

7. Would you be interested in reading other *Heartsong Presents* titles?   ❏ Yes   ❏ No

8. Please check your age range:
❏ Under 18   ❏ 18-24   ❏ 25-34
❏ 35-45   ❏ 46-55   ❏ Over 55

9. How many hours per week do you read? ————

Name _____

Occupation _____

Address _____

City _____ State _____ Zip _____

Don't miss these favorite Heartsong Presents *titles
by some of our most distinguished authors!*

Your price is only $2.95 each!

___HP01 A TORCH FOR TRINITY, *Colleen L. Reece*
___HP02 WILDFLOWER HARVEST, *Colleen L. Reece*
___HP03 RESTORE THE JOY, *Sara Mitchell*
___HP04 REFLECTIONS OF THE HEART, *Sally Laity*
___HP10 SONG OF LAUGHTER, *Lauraine Snelling*
___HP17 LLAMA LADY, *VeraLee Wiggins*
___HP18 ESCORT HOMEWARD, *Eileen M. Berger*
___HP19 A PLACE TO BELONG, *Janelle Jamison*
___HP23 GONE WEST, *Kathleen Karr*
___HP28 DAKOTA DAWN, *Lauraine Snelling*
___HP36 THE SURE PROMISE, *JoAnn A. Grote*
___HP39 GOVERNOR'S DAUGHTER, *Veda Boyd Jones*
___HP41 FIELDS OF SWEET CONTENT, *Norma Jean Lutz*
___HP42 SEARCH FOR TOMORROW, *Mary Hawkins*
___HP43 VEILED JOY, *Colleen L. Reece*
___HP44 DAKOTA DREAM, *Lauraine Snelling*

······ Presents ······

Great Inspirational Romance at a Great Price!

Heartsong Presents books are inspirational romances in contemporary and historical settings, designed to give you an enjoyable, spirit-lifting reading experience. You can choose from 92 wonderfully written titles from some of today's best authors like Colleen L. Reece, Brenda Bancroft, Janelle Jamison, and many others.

When ordering quantities less than twelve, above titles are $2.95 each.

SEND TO: Heartsong Presents Reader's Service
P.O. Box 719, Uhrichsville, Ohio 44683

Please send me the items checked above. I am enclosing $_____.
(please add $1.00 to cover postage per order. OH add 6.25% tax. NJ add 6%.). Send check or money order, no cash or C.O.D.s, please.
To place a credit card order, call 1-800-847-8270.

NAME _____

ADDRESS _____

CITY/STATE_____ ZIP _____

LOVE A GREAT LOVE STORY?
Introducing Heartsong Presents —
Your Inspirational Book Club

Heartsong Presents Christian romance reader's service will provide you with four never before published romance titles every month! In fact, your books will be mailed to you at the same time advance copies are sent to book reviewers. You'll preview each of these new and unabridged books before they are released to the general public.

These books are filled with the kind of stories you have been longing for—stories of courtship, chivalry, honor, and virtue. Strong characters and riveting plot lines will make you want to read on and on. Romance is not dead, and each of these romantic tales will remind you that Christian faith is still the vital ingredient in an intimate relationship filled with true love and honest devotion.

Sign up today to receive your first set. Send no money now. We'll bill you only $9.97 post-paid with your shipment. Then every month you'll automatically receive the latest four "hot off the press" titles for the same low post-paid price of $9.97. That's a savings of 50% off the $4.95 cover price. When you consider the exaggerated shipping charges of other book clubs, your savings are even greater!

THERE IS NO RISK—you may cancel at any time without obligation. And if you aren't completely satisfied with any selection, return it for an immediate refund.

TO JOIN, just complete the coupon below, mail it today, and get ready for hours of wholesome entertainment.

Now you can curl up, relax, and enjoy some great reading full of the warmhearted spirit of romance.